PRIDE

Love is Cure, Vol. 1 - Vices & Virtues Series

Book One

Brookelyn Mosley

85 Media LLC

Pride
Love is Cure Series, Vol. 1 - Vices & Virtues Series
Book One
© 2020 Brookelyn Mosley. All rights reserved.

ISBN (eBook): 978-1-965507-06-3

ISBN (Paperback): 978-1-965507-07-0

First Edition: November 2020

Cover Design by Brookelyn Mosley

Published by 85 Media LLC

BrookelynMosley.com

Printed in the United States of America

More By Brookelyn Mosley

Links to the below stories can be found here (https://brookelynmosley.com/ebooks-paperbacks/)

Novels/Novellas/Novelettes/Series

- No Fraternizing, Pt. 1
- No Fraternizing, Pt. 2
- No Fraternizing, Pt. 3
- First Came Love: The Love, Hate & Revenge Prequel
- Love, Hate & Revenge, Pt. 1
- Love, Hate & Revenge, Pt. 2
- Love, Hate & Revenge, Pt. 3
- Girl Code
- Mr. & Mrs. Jones
- Forbidden: An Anthology
- They Call Me Mello
- A Love Deferred
- Indecent Arrangement
- Last Comes Love
- Ebb & Flow
- PRIDE
- Meant To Be
- LUST
- Loveless
- GREED
- Rekindled
- My First, My Last

• ENVY
• Ready or Not
• So This is Love
• Home Before Midnight
• GLUTTONY
• When Luke Met Juliette
• When Life Gives You Sunsets
• In Love, I Trust
• WRATH
• SLOTH

Short Stories
• Unsilent Knight
• Twice In Love
• Home For Christmas

ByBK Exclusives

Bed Bully

Stuck

LHR Rewind Series

Home Before Midnight

Maybe This Time Will Be Different

Lovekilla

Incoming Call

Rough

WYD

Drinks on Me

Cali & Lee

Ray & Jay

Living Out a Love Song

Glimpses

One Mic

With Love, Ayanna & Dallas

Just Friends

Lena's Ex-File

Dream Boss

Chateau Luxure

Click Here to see if new exclusive shorts have been added to ByBK
(Copy + paste this link if the above link doesn't work: https://
bybrookelynmosley.com/collections/ebooks)

Acknowledgments

A loving thank you to my amazing husband who is without a doubt one of my biggest supporters. Your support is worth its weight in gold. A special thank you to my reading family. To the active members in my Facebook reading group, my beloved beta readers for this project, and my supporters across all social medias. You all have embraced my brand of writing and I'm beyond appreciative of it. Shout out to the readers who have reached out to me to share your thoughts regarding my books. I thank you for keeping me motivated and excited to create new projects for you. When I write, I keep you in mind. Thank you for your support. It's my soul food.

Dedicated to the saints and the sinners...

ONE

"Ugh, *what* am I even doing here?"

My heels clicked and clacked against the school's polished floors beneath me as I made my way toward music that hammered out of floor speakers.

"You two know I'm above this, right? Like, one million miles above this, right?"

This would be the last time I walked these halls, with my girls Moni and Kasha, after graduation the next morning.

"Let's not stay long, I beg," I said to them as I led the way toward our pre-graduation party.

Well, it wasn't *our* pre-graduation party per se. It was a soiree for all graduating seniors, hosted by members of one of the school's fraternities, one of the popular Greek fraternities on campus. Every guy at *LU* wanted to bark like a dog while stomping on the floor, doing what they did that made heads turn in their direction. Similar to how my girls reacted whenever they were around those frat boys, to my annoyance.

"*Ugh,*" I groaned as we turned the corner and the music's volume grew louder. "I sure hope this won't be the only genre blasted this evening."

"Damn, Summer," Moni whined behind me. "Will you stop

complaining? Please don't be like that tonight." She wrapped an arm around my shoulder and pulled me into a side hug. "This is our last night as Langstoners. Let's make it a good time, yeah?"

I kissed my teeth.

"But this isn't my scene at all." I pouted and stomped my foot. "The only reason I'm here is because you begged me to come. I want you to know that."

"Not my scene either," Kasha said to the right of me. She pulled out a hand mirror from her bag and held it up to her mouth, blotting her matted purple lips together to renew the color. "But I have to get laid tonight. Once my law internship begins in Philly a week from today, I'll have no time for dick."

I snorted a laugh.

"Probably won't even have time to call y'all."

"I'm backpacking through Europe so I wouldn't know a thing about that." Moni winked a hazel-eye. "Let's all go in here and have a good time, anyway though, 'kay?"

"You only want to *go in here* for Roman, so save it, *'kay*?" I teased, poking her at the side. She pushed my hand away while giggling. "You've been ogling that guy since the start of your freshman year. Maybe you've found the balls to jump his bones tonight so you can put us all out of our miseries."

Kasha laughed.

Moni pulled me by the arm. "Whatever, let's go."

We'd reach the tall wooden door that led down to the lower level of the school. I was familiar with this side of campus. Spent a lot of time here during my enrollment at *LU*, throwing parties and hosting charity events like food and coat drives for the homeless. My mother believed hosting events like the aforementioned was a waste of effort, insisting I do something better with my time. But I loved organizing charitable events at *LU*. I never admitted that to her though. I'd never hear the end of it if I did.

Anyway, tonight, the frat boys planned to sully the basement with cheap liquor and bass-filled hip hop music.

"*Ugh*," I groaned again, but this time to myself.

The moment we arrived at the bottom of the steps and entered through the heavy wooden door, my eyes scanned the place and the people in it.

Girls with barely there outfits, platform stripper heels so high *my* feet hurt staring at them.

Guys in purple shirts swarmed the place like killer bees. Those were the frat boys, the ones responsible for the party.

"What up ladies," one greeted the moment we stepped inside. I recognized him as one of the frat brothers. He dressed himself in their signature royal purple and old gold with the frat's Greek letters etched down the fabric of his sweater. "So, we got cups set up on the left and drinks on the right of them."

I glanced that way and rolled my eyes back over to him.

"Why are there two different colored cups?" Moni asked what I was thinking.

The guy grinned. "Red for taken and green for single."

"I'm sorry?" I questioned.

"Relationship status'," he replied with a smirk. "Get it? Red for *stop right there*, green for *come and get it*."

I scoffed. "Ew, you *must* be kidding me."

His eyes crinkled at the corners when he swiped his tongue over his bottom lip. "Summer, right?"

I didn't bother to respond.

He moved closer, leaned in, and said in my ear, "I'll be watching closely to see what cup you pick up." He stepped back and winked at me before turning to walk away.

"That's a hard no," I said to my girls, flipping my hair over my shoulder. "I can tell I'll need a soak in ammonia with a touch of acid after this horrid shindig, yuck."

"Okay, Summer?" Kasha scolded behind me. "You're going to have to put the claws away tonight, kitty cat, and play nice with the dogs."

"Whatever." I inhaled a calming breath while pushing my *LV* bag up my arm, hooking the leather handle behind my elbow. "Let's get this over with already."

We approached the table, and all picked up green cups. I was tempted to choose red just to ensure none of these hooligans approached me but knew my girls would lambaste me for not being a good sport. My hand wrapped around the neck of the only wine bottle on the table. There was no whiskey, which I preferred, only cognac, gin, and vodka, so I had to settle for the wine since I hated the others. But when I lifted the bottle to read the label, I grimaced.

"*Barefoot Moscato*?!" I asked out loud. "This frat is the most illustrious fraternity on campus and they're serving *Barefoot Moscato*?"

"What are you even saying right now?! I love this one. It's my favorite!" Moni said beside me, taking it out of my hand. "Give it here."

I dropped my head back between my shoulders in defeat and grunted, my hair feathering down my bare back exposed by my halter top. "Is it time to go yet?"

"You just got here though," a deep voice said to my left.

I peered over at him and his eyes pulled me in.

Jayce Martin.

This six-foot-something guy was a living god. Every girl on campus wanted a moment of his time, if not his full undivided attention. Although, I'm sure, most of them wouldn't mind sharing. He didn't have to do much to get that kind of fanfare besides breathe.

My view instinctively fell on his lips. His body was what the girls around campus lusted over, but his mouth was my favorite thing to admire from a discreet distance. Full, thick, and shaped like Cupid's bow at the top. The dip became even more pronounced when he smiled like how he did in that moment. And his teeth, *oh God*, his teeth were like perfectly shaped piano keys that made my heart sing. For almost half a decade, whenever I encountered him on campus, his eyes always dug into me. They made me blissfully uncomfortable and sent other sensations racing through me.

"Yup, just got here," I answered, as cool and calm as I could. "And already I've been here way too long." I swept my eyes up and down his tall frame, then turned my gaze on my girls. "Ladies?" I gestured with my head to walk away.

He chuckled, "Y'all enjoy yourselves tonight, aight?"

My pulse galloped as I passed him. He always smelled so good. It was clear that wasn't cologne he wore. Probably fragrance oil or some variation.

"Jayce is feeling you," Moni said to me the moment we pulled out chairs at a lone table in a corner and took our seats. "He looks at you different, gives you all of his attention when he talks to you. I haven't seen him pay that much attention to any other girls on campus the way he does with you."

"Didn't notice and don't care." I took a sip of the wine from my green party cup and cringed. "This drink is terrible. Now if *I* threw this party, there would be champagne sitting on ice in buckets, crystal flutes instead of these color coded catcalling cups, and R&B... *yes*, slow jams, softly humming from the speakers. We shouldn't have to yell over each other to have a proper conversation."

"Well, I like this." Moni shrugged.

"You would," I replied.

Moni waved her hand in the air as if to say whatever.

Not even an hour into the event, the frat brothers got into position.

"And here we go," I mumbled.

The men gathered at the center of the room, stomped, hopped, and shouted in unison, forming a snake line that spanned from one end of the room to the next. Barking rang out around us. The typical scene at one of these parties.

"I don't understand why they have to do this everywhere they are," I said to myself.

My eyes searched for *him* though. I couldn't believe myself. But there was something about Jayce that drew me to him, no matter how hard I tried not to care.

I found him near the center of the line. His tongue hung out of his mouth as he oscillated his neck, framed his face with twisted wrists, and hopped around with the rest of the members. Jeans slung low, hat turned to the back. My mother would *die* if I ever brought someone like him home with me.

Yet and still I couldn't stop my body from reacting to his antics.

I first laid eyes on Jayce during freshman orientation four years prior. He was there with the other frat boys doing nothing at all besides scoping. Probably tallying up who they planned to invite into their rooms before the semester even started.

It was a late August morning. The earliest I'd woken up since begin-

ning summer vacation. Move in day happened the day before so I was all set up in my dorm room.

I walked along the halls of LU, the only student with a purse instead of a backpack. Who cared? I'd just gotten this Valentino crossbody bag my mother insisted I bring with me on campus, and I wanted to wear it because it matched my maroon suede booties.

The moment I turned the corner, heading to the doors of the gym, I saw him. Jayce stood tall against a wall surrounded by other guys, but I saw no one else but him. He had one leg hiked up, his foot pressed against the wall behind him. He buried his hands in his jeans' pockets and kept a blue Yankee's baseball cap on his head that was positioned low, the lid casting a shadow over his eyes. All he wore was a tee and jeans, denim that practically hung off his ass exposing his designer label boxers. On his feet were wheat-colored construction Timberland boots with the tongues flipped out.

My mother warned me about boys like Jayce. That was one of the reasons she hesitated with agreeing for me to attend LU. The university was a top private university in the country known as a basketball school. So it attracted a lot of Jayce's kind who attended on full basketball scholarships. For months before I moved on campus, my mother insisted I stay far away from boys like him, "the inner city types" as she called them. She made me promise to exchange as little words with them as possible. But there was something about Jayce that kept my eyes glued to him... and his to me.

He slid his tongue out his mouth long enough to lick his thick lips slow when he caught me staring. I turned my head away quickly the second the walls inside me pulled in. When I glanced at him once again, he winked at me.

"Nope," I said to him out loud, and that made him laugh.

His laugh was sexy, made him even more attractive as if that was even possible. From that day on, I knew the hardest thing about being in college wouldn't be the classes. Maintaining a distance from him would be the challenge.

"I hear he's graduating summa cum laude." Kasha said, drawing me out of my thoughts.

I darted my eyes in her direction. "Who?"

She pointed. "Jayce."

"Puh-lease." I snorted. "Impossible."

"Just because he plays basketball for the school and is in a frat doesn't mean he can't be smart too, Summer," Moni defended.

"Oh, yes it does."

Moni snickered. "You're such a bitch."

"There's no way he's graduating summa cum laude. *I'm* graduating summa cum laude."

Moni shrugged. "And?"

"*And...* I worked hard to do that. Jayce over there..." I pointed. "... probably paid good money to have people take the tests that got him good grades. No way on earth he earned that. I'm certain of it. This is ridiculous."

"She might have a point there," Kasha chimed in. "I heard he slept with three of his professors and a handful of teacher aides."

"And I heard the same thing," I added.

"Whatever." Moni pushed her chair back to stand up. "You two are acting like two old hags sitting on a stoop, just serial killing my vibe. I'm going to work the room."

"Yeah, to find Roman so you can stack your green cup with his, right?" I giggled. "Didn't I call it, Kasha?"

"Bye!" Moni shouted as she walked away.

"Summa cum laude, huh?" I asked Kasha, and she nodded.

I twisted my lips to one side. "Hmph."

"Do you *want* him now?"

I glanced at her to find her wiggling her threaded brows. A sly grin played on her purple lips. I balled mine in response.

"Please Kasha, you know me better than that." I took another sip of my drink, cringed, then swallowed hard. "I could *never* be with a man like Jayce."

Two

JAYCE

"Jayce baby, come on!" my mother yelled from the living room.

"I'll be out in three minutes."

I stood in front of the floor-length mirror that leaned against the wall, adjusting my purple tie around my neck. It was graduation day. A day I'd been dreaming about since I received my acceptance letter in the mail from LU.

"Traffic is not good at this hour Jayce and I do not want you to be late."

I grunted as I crouched down to tie the laces on my gold-painted boots with my frat's Greek letters painted down the sides in purple. My frat brothers deserved most of the credit for keeping me focused and on track to see this day.

"Boy, get yo' ass in this living room right now before I have to come in there and drag you out by your damn ear!"

"This woman." I kissed my teeth and turned to leave my room. "Talkin' to me like I'm still a teenager."

I walked out to my mother standing in the middle of the living room holding up my royal blue graduation cap and gown.

"Aww, check out my baby," she gushed, her eyes welling with tears.

"Your baby, huh? Weren't you just hollering for me to get my ass out here while threatening me?"

She giggled as she approached me to fix my tie. "Your father would be so proud of you, Jayce. Here." She handed me my gown. "Summa cum laude! That's *my* baby!"

I laughed.

My twin brother and sister waited on the couch, their eyes down on their phones, disinterested. Typical fifteen-year-old shit. I didn't expect them to see how major this was.

The first in the family to graduate college and with top honors. I received a full ride scholarship to attend *Langston University* and to play ball for the school. Made sure my grades remained perfect so that scholarship money would continue to roll in every year. Stayed an extra year at *LU* for that purpose. My good grades was the only reason they continued to pay out *Langston University's* growing tuition costs. Between juggling side hustles, maintaining good grades, playing basketball for *LU*, fulfilling my obligations to my frat, *and* watching over my baby brother and sister, I wasn't trying to risk it by taking on too many classes every semester. So, I opted for a 5-year graduation plan instead of aiming to graduate in four. And I don't regret my decision. Attending school and getting good grades was never only for me, anyway. It was for my family. We needed this win.

"Let me see you," my mother insisted, turning me by the shoulders. "Oooh, you are so handsome."

"Thanks mama." I leaned forward to give her a kiss on the cheek.

"Okay." My mother clapped her hands together. "Let's go y'all."

The moment we stepped out of our apartment, the earthy scent of weed hit us right in the face.

We screwed up our faces like we always did, my sister pinching her nose closed as we continued pacing toward the elevator, inhaling as little air as possible to keep from passing out. Thankfully, the elevator was working that morning.

I grew up in *Stuyvesant Houses*, one of the many projects in Brooklyn... one of the oldest actually. This was a public housing you moved into and rarely moved out of until you died. I knew people who have never stepped a foot outside of the neighborhood, much less the state.

After starting school at *LU* on a basketball scholarship, I could have lived on campus, but I stayed home. My siblings weren't old enough to take care of themselves and I already knew what life out here could be like for impressionable kids, especially a black boy and girl with a mother who worked all the time.

As we rode down in the elevator, I kept my focus forward. In about a week, I'd be moving into my own place at the insistence of my mother.

"Jayce, you're grown now," she told me one morning, two months before graduation. "You have enough leftover from your scholarship money saved up to get your own place. The time has arrived for you to spread your wings. The experience of living on your own is essential to your life as a man."

So I took her advice and found a studio apartment in Harlem. I chose the city because of the summer internship I'd landed a few months back that started in a few weeks.

Outside, I unlocked the doors of my black Camry, and we all hopped in.

The car was a high school graduation gift from my mother. She worked extra hours and took on a part-time job at a gourmet market to get it for me. When she gifted it, I refused to take it. Then she threatened to beat my ass for being difficult and gave me no choice but to accept. That was my mother. Mrs. Mariah Martin. Tough as nails, but sweet as pie. Gotta love her.

Behind the wheel, I stroked my pretty boy goatee, deep in thought. My eyes remained fixed ahead on the road when my mother asked, "What you over there thinking about?"

I glanced at her.

My mother was stunning. Smooth butter brown skin framed by naturally rolled black locs that hung to the middle of her back. She looked tired, she always looked tired. Working over time at a demanding job at the city's clerk office as a receptionist will do that to you. But again, that was my mother, a hard worker. Someone who sacrificed for her family and never complained about it.

"I'm thinking about the house I showed you the other day online," I answered.

"Jayce, baby, don't start this again."

"I'm serious about getting you that house mama," I insisted. "You, Shanae, and Shane would live comfortable in that spot. It's in a dope neighborhood and close to the trains."

"Jayce—"

"I gotta get y'all out the projects."

"Why is this the focus of conversation on your graduation day?"

"Because it's always been *my* focus, ma."

I braked softly at the red light and I turned to her. "Just *please* go check out the open house with me."

"For what?!" she damn near hollered. "I can't afford no place like that and I know your non-working-about-to-graduate-college self can't either."

I bit my tongue to keep from responding. Little did she know I was doing more than just hitting the books and the courts while at school these past five years.

"Just check it out," I insisted.

"I'm not getting into this with you today." She tossed her locs over her shoulder and focused out the windshield. "The light is green."

I kissed my teeth, faced forward, lifted my foot off the brake pedal, and gave the car a little gas.

One expressway and a bridge later, we arrived at the university. I parked in the student parking lot and hopped out the car, ironing out the wrinkles in my gown using my hand.

"Here's your stole and honor cords." She beamed, draping first the purple and blue cords around my neck, then the double gold ones, before laying my purple and gold kente stole, with my frat's letters of course, over the cords. "Oh my goodness!"

I scoffed a laugh. "Ma, you gotta chill."

"Oh, hush. Shane, Shanae," she called to my twin siblings. "Get over here so I can get this picture with you all."

We stood in front of the car, smiling, making silly faces, and my mother cackled as she snapped pictures on her phone.

In my peripheral, I spotted movement and saw *her* walking past us with a woman at her side.

Her long dark hair blew in the wind like a 90s Pantene commercial as she strutted by, cat-shaped eyes boring into me, not at all trying to break eye contact first.

I tossed my chin up, my way of saying hey, and she averted her eyes away from me immediately.

"Stuck up ass," I mumbled to myself, fighting back my smile. I turned to my family and told them, "Let's go y'all."

The school arranged for the graduation to occur in the school's gym. *Langston University's* school gym was one of the largest, if not *the* largest, school gym on the east coast. It was close to the size of an arena. We took basketball seriously at *LU*.

"Damn, I'm gonna miss this place," I whispered to myself.

"Lookin' sharp player," my boy and teammate, Townsend, said behind me.

"Ayyeee!" I hollered, pulling him into a hug. "Congratulations my dude! We made it."

"Congrats to you, too." He stepped back and clapped his hands. "And yes we did."

"So, what's up?" I asked, as we made our way to the back where all the graduates were lining up. "You hitting up any parties with us after this?"

"Yup, yup, you know this," he sang.

I tossed my head back and laughed. When I leveled my dome to scan the room to find more familiar faces, my eyes fell on *her* again.

Ms. Summer McKoy. Shorty was so bad. Soft tawny skin, big porcelain doll eyes, but hers slanted upward like a feline's. She had a heart-shaped face with a sharp chin and her sexy lips always, and I mean always formed a pout. I don't think the girl ever smiled, but she was pretty as hell and the only female on campus who never gave me the chance of day. I liked that shit. She did not understand how much I liked a challenge. I just couldn't stand her attitude.

Stuck up ass.

She walked my way followed by two other girls, one with light eyes and the other an Indian and black girl. They always hung out as a trio. It was cute. She was cute. So damn cute.

"So, you *are* graduating summa cum laude," Summer said, her eyes fixed on the honor cords' tassels I wore over my gown and beneath my frat's purple and gold stole. Her gown was open with double silver and gold honor cords draped over both her shoulders. But honestly, I barely glanced at those cords because my eyes couldn't pull away from her breasts, hips, or legs. Her pale pink dress was tight, appeared painted on. Summer's legs glistened under the overhead lights. I had to force my eyes off them.

"And so are you," I replied. "It must be my very special day for real though, huh? Ms. Summer McKoy is initiating conversation with *me*."

A hint of a smile pulled at her lips.

"And wait, hold up," I teased, closing the space between us, crouching down just a little to be at eye level with her. "Did I almost make her smile too? I'm on a roll."

She pursed her lips together, doing her best to fight back her grin.

With her eyes still on me, she told her girls, "Come on ladies. Let's go get in position to march."

I followed her with my eyes as she walked away, trying my hardest to see that fat ass of hers through the fabric of her graduation gown.

Townsend whistled next to me. "She *knows* she's fine."

"I know right?" I replied, still watching her. "I can't stand her sexy ass."

Townsend crouched over laughing.

"Let's go do this man." I reached my hand out in front of me for a dap from Townsend, which he met. "My mother will kill me if she doesn't see my ass in position to walk to our seats so she can get yet another shot of me in this gown."

"Aight," Townsend acknowledged beside me. "So, when do you start your internship?"

"June 3rd," I answered, moving toward the large flag that represented the school's law program. "In three weeks."

"A summer law internship," Townsend said. I turned to him to find him with his tongue hanging out his mouth. The scene made me snort a laugh.

"If I wasn't traveling this summer," he added, "I'd be in one before starting law school in the fall. Can you imagine all the fine ass interns that'll be posted up in there?"

"Doubt that," I replied, leaning against the wall. Members of the school band were getting in position to play - the school's way of ushering us into the ceremony in *Langston U* style. "I'm not expecting any of them to look at all decent."

"For real?"

"For real," I parroted. "This summer internship is for the nerdy and ambitious. There will be no eye candy within sight. I'm almost sure of that."

Three

My heels smacked against the polished floors of *Brown, Bloom & Associates*. It was my first day of my law internship and I was two minutes late.

The fucking train.

"Now, that sounds like an excuse, doll," I could hear my mother reminding me in my head.

"Ugh," I groaned to myself.

Not being on time would ruin everything. First impressions mattered so much to me. People formed them and never forgot them, regardless of how hard you worked to convince them otherwise.

For the morning, I sported a yellow crepe midi-dress that stopped right below my knees. On top of that was my tailor-made olive green blazer and the matching scalloped collar stiletto heels on my feet. I looked cute. Not just lawyer cute. Real cute. Couldn't keep my eyes from drifting to any reflection of me I could find on the way here. On a perfect day, I would nail my first day. Not being two minutes late though.

"Fucking train," I spat, turning the corner and heading straight to the receptionist desk. "Can you tell me where the east wing conference room is?"

I'd received the email last night detailing where I would meet with the other interns for orientation. *Brown, Bloom & Associates'* summer internship program was the most coveted at the university, in the country actually.

Everyone who was anyone knew *Langston U* as the school that produced some of the best writers thanks to the university's namesake. But second in line for the ideal major to study at *LU* was law. Their program was the best in the state. I've wanted to be a lawyer after watching only one episode of *Living Single*. It was a show that premiered years before my birth, but my mother loved viewing the taped shows in our TV room on VHS. The moment Maxine Shaw stepped onto the screen, I knew exactly what I wanted to be when I grew up.

Not being two minutes late though.

Yes, *two minute*s. I'm making a big fuss over two measly minutes because I just knew my mother would.

I headed in the direction the receptionist pointed, and when I slid opened the door, there sat other people. They all looked my age or around my age box all accept this one guy who could easily pass for thirty.

All eyes settled on me when I walked in, but mine zeroed in on the two vacant chairs.

I let out a long sigh of relief. Usually, I could give two damns and no shits what everyone else was doing but seeing that one other empty chair took the burden off of being the only late person.

My eyes scanned the room once again, recording the faces to memory. There was an equal share of gender in the room. That had to be strategic. Three men and three women. I made four, which meant empty chair over there would seat the fourth man.

"Good morning is a good start," I addressed the room when the stares continued without a word spoken.

I strutted over to the head of the table to snag the seat there.

"*You* walked into the room," one girl sassed. She had this creamy dark brown skin that glowed. Her eyes were even darker and sharp. She was pretty... not prettier than me though. "You should be the one to greet us," she added.

I pursed my lips. "Wish harder."

My eyes rolled away from hers, focusing forward at the other end of the table and on the empty chair.

I pointed. "I see another intern is tardy."

"Nope. You're the *only* one late," Ms. Thang disclosed. "*He* was actually the first one here. He stepped out for a drink of water."

"Oh." I pouted, then shrugged. "Doesn't matter, anyway."

"Why do you say that?" one of the gentlemen inquired.

Because my mother knows a few of the partners here personally and all I have to do is show up and stay for the entire internship and the job is mine. Na-nana-na-na. Losers.

"No reason," I bristled instead.

The door sliding opened pulled our attentions in that direction.

My jaw almost hit the floor when *he* walked in.

Intricate full bow-like lips, piercing caramel browns boring into me. Used to seeing him in jeans, a tee, and a hat turned backwards, the Adonis nearly knocked me out my seat as my eyes digested him from head to toe. Three-piece designer suit fitted to his physique or maybe he was just that put together physically that clothes laid against his frame as if he were a walking breathing mannequin.

His jaw dropped too as he paused in step for only a moment. His shoes caught the ceiling lights adding the right sparkle to send his sexy through the Richter scale measuring the quaking of my thighs.

Shit, shit, shit!

"What the *fuck*?!" I said loud.

"Whoa!" Jayce smiled with all of his teeth. "Language, Ms. McKoy."

Ms. Thang pointed back and forth between us. "You two *know* each other."

"Oh my God." I threw my head back between my shoulders. "This is *not* happening."

"Okay, fresh blood," a man announced while stepping through the conference door. I leveled my head to focus on the graying 50-something black man who'd entered the room. In tow was a petite blonde with a yellow notepad and black pen in her grip. "Welcome to the first day of your lives."

My eyes drifted over to Jayce to see him still perusing all of me while wearing that smirk that secretly drove me all kinds of wild.

"I'm Jeff Taylor, but you can call me J or JT. I will *never* answer to Mr. Taylor and if you *ever* call me that, you will move to the very top of my can't-sit-with-me shit list, understood?"

We all nodded.

"Perfect. You lucky eight are here to compete for the *one and only* position that we're offering to the standout, outstanding intern who leaves a lasting impression. The chosen one will receive their own desk and a beautiful ten thousand dollar sign-on bonus. A bonus damn near unheard of in our industry and rarely, if ever, offered to law students still wet behind the ears like you eight."

I ran my hands through my hair, tossing the black strands back between my shoulders and refusing to hold back my smile. With little effort, I allowed my mind to escape to a wonderland of thoughts, filled with racks and racks of designer labels that I'd be able to splurge on once my sign-on bonus cleared. The job was *so* mine.

"There's only room for one," Jeff emphasized, placing his hand at his chubby waist. "This is not your mother's internship. You will not get me coffee, answer my phone, or make me copies. You will, however, get real courtroom experience. Be right there beside us in the thick of things. Smell lady justice up close. So, here are a few tips - I don't like suck-ups, I abhor excuses, and tardiness..." He peered over at me. "... will not be tolerated after today."

My smile melted into a frown instantly.

"In the permanent position, I want a scholar who is able to problem solve fast, be an even faster critical thinker than me, land on their feet, and offer not okay, not good, but supremely *excellent* results every single time, no exceptions. I don't do recommendation letters so if you don't get the job, you *don't* get the goddamn job, and I will *not* help you get another one. Is that also understood?"

"Yes," the room asserted in unison.

"Great." Jeff moved to the front of the room. "I am not your friend, your brother, your father, or your uncle so don't expect me to be. I do not own, nor do I fit any kiddie gloves. Pay attention to what I say, watch what I do, and take plenty of notes. This floor of *Brown, Bloom, & Associa*tes specializes in criminal law. We'll be dealing with some of the most contradicting clientele that are sometimes rotten pieces of shits who are often the mold on top of mold but *you* will carry yourselves with integrity and with a focus on achieving desired results to win our case, no matter what. Is *that* understood?"

"Shit," I mumbled.

Jeff whipped his head in my direction.

"I mean." I perked up in my seat. "Yes, understood."

"Wonderful." He clapped his hands once, then pointed at all of us. "All of you, exchange numbers. You'll be working closely with one another and will need to relay information between the eight of you if I deliver it once to one of you. I absolutely *hate* repeating myself so staying in contact with each other is helpful to remain in the loop and not get left behind."

My eyes roamed over at Jayce to see him holding his phone up, waving it from side to side at me.

I released a frustrated sigh.

"That's it," Jeff concluded, making his way to the door. "*That* was orientation. Short and to the point. You're welcome. And this is Stephanie." He pointed at the petite blonde who followed him into the conference room.

We all focused on her.

"Hey guys," she greeted with a sweet smile.

"She's my legal assistant. This will be your point of contact before even uttering so much as a word to me. She looks adorable like a teacup Maltese, but don't let that fool you. That's just her face, Steph can't help that. But she's a Rottweiler. Treat her good or she'll handle you with her manicured claws without a single protest from me."

Stephanie shook her head modestly while holding up a sympathetic hand.

"See you all tomorrow morning, bright and early." He turned to glare at me. "And on time."

I forced the warmest smile my lips could support in that moment.

"Okay guys," Stephanie said, following Jeff out. "See you all in the morning."

"718," I began. "555-2933. You can all just text me yours."

I coiled my fingers around the handle of my bag. "I'm out of here."

"The last number..." Jayce tried from his seat across the table. *God, he's so sexy.* "... was that a three you said?"

"Yes," I growled. I pushed my chair back and stood up.

"And your name?" one intern asked. "We should at least exchange names before you go."

"It's Summer," Jayce said for me. "Charming name, not so much of a kind person though."

"Fine." I plopped my bag down onto the table and it made a loud thud. "What is *everyone's* name?"

"Carter," the thirty-something gentleman said.

"I'm Rolanda," the squeaky-voice pixie cut one announced.

"Veronika," the dark-skin beauty who sassed me when I walked in earlier affirmed.

"David," the lanky biracial guy with the crooked glasses stated.

"Morrison," the petite stud with too tight of a suit introduced next.

"Xiomara," the only Latin girl in the room chirped with the roll of her tongue.

"And I'm Jayce y'all," he announced, his voice heavy with bass. "It's a pleasure to meet all of you."

"So, how do you two know each other?" Veronika asked Jayce, pointing at me.

"We attended the same school, *Langston U,*" he answered, his eyes on me. "Just graduated."

"Well..." I batted my eyelashes. "*I* graduated *on* schedule. Jayce here had to spend an extra year at *LU.*"

"By choice," he added.

"So *you* say."

He laughed. "I'm surprised you knew *that* much about me."

"Anyway," I said, grabbing my bag again, realizing my blunder, "I will see you all tomorrow, I guess."

"I wonder where they'll host our welcome dinner," Rolanda queried to the group.

"Welcome dinner?" I asked.

"Yep." She leaned in my direction. "*Brown, Bloom & Associates* are infamous for hosting the most amazing welcome dinners for their interns. Whether you get the job or not, you at least get to experience class on their dime."

"*Ugh.*" I rolled my eyes. "We have to eat together, too?"

Jayce snorted a laugh.

Veronika scoffed, her lip cocked at one side in disgust. "Eww, whatever!"

Jayce's snort became a boisterous laugh.

"I take it we're all done here, so bye," I said as I approached the door and exited the room.

I couldn't escape fast enough from that bunch. If I could be honest, the seven of them in that room probably knew more about *Brown, Bloom & Associates* than I did. I just knew I wanted to work there because my father held *BBA* in high regard. He sought the help of one of their attorneys often, one who specialized in business law, in matters dealing with his real estate business.

My dad, Steven McKoy, was dubbed the king of New York because of all the buildings he owned and sold around the state. He worked so much I barely saw him. Haven't seen him in ten years actually, even though we live only a toll and tunnel away. Hadn't realized it's been that long since we've spoken, but that's neither here nor there.

"Summer," I heard behind me.

When I turned toward the voice, I saw Jayce swaggering my way. "What do you want?"

He smiled that dreamy smile of his. "Can we put this little cat and dog vibe we got going on here to rest and play nice for the next two months?"

"What for?" I slid my bag off one arm and onto the other as I leaned to the side to press the elevator's call button. "I'm not *here* to make friends. We're competing for a position. Even though you're really no competition."

"I'm not?"

"Of course you're not. Look, I don't understand how you got here but you *have* to know you don't belong."

"Damn, Summer. I'm crushed." He wore a smile the whole time. To add insult to injury, he pressed his hand to his chest, faking offense. "Why would you say such a thing like that to me?"

I grunted. "How did you graduate summa cum laude, Jayce? Huh? How? How are *you* here competing for an internship that only accepts eight people out of thousands of applicants?" I stomped my foot and sneered through my teeth, "Tell me how and right now!"

He chuckled, and that only ticked me off more.

"Jayce, I busted my *ass* for four years, including enrolling in summer school just to graduate on time. I had the under eye bags that I needed to cover with layers and *layers* of concealer to show for my sacrifice. *You?*" I groaned, really wanting to scream. "You dribbled a ball up and down a gym, stomped the yard with your dogs, and graduated late. You being here with me just doesn't make sense." I gasped and pointed his way when a thought occurred to me. "That's it, isn't it? Your fraternity. It has to be! I know you guys *hook each other up* like that," I said with finger quotes.

Jayce responded with nothing. He just folded his bottom lip into his mouth and bit down on it.

I shifted my eyes away and exhaled in defeat.

"I'll be happy to share all of that with you at the welcome dinner..." He moved in closer. "... or privately if you want to know sooner."

His mother must have dipped him in a slow cooked batter of sexy at some point in his life because the guy oozed that shit to my annoyance.

I wouldn't be able to focus with him here. It was hard enough getting through those semesters when we'd pass each other in the halls and I fought the urge to pull him into my dorm room by his pullover's hood. No. I wouldn't be able to focus. Not without getting him out of my system.

I'll have to fuck him. With hope, he's terrible in bed.

No doll, my mother's voice echoed in the corners of my mind. *Don't you dare!*

The elevator doors slid opened behind me just in time, and I sighed with relief.

Once inside I told him, "If I were you, I wouldn't waste my time giving it my all here. Don't even bother getting comfortable because you probably won't be here long."

He stepped one foot in the car, obstructing the doors from closing.

"Because the job is mine," I added.

"How you figured that?"

"My mother put in a good word for me," I revealed, lifting my chin with an air of arrogance. "All I have to do is show up, and the job is mine. So..." I approached him and pressed my hand against his chest to push him back and off the car so the elevator doors would close. But when I did, he didn't budge. He arrested me with his gaze and smelled divine doing it. The hard muscle of his pec felt so good against my fingertips. I slid my fingers down his chest slowly before snatching my hand off him once I realized what I was doing.

"You have fun jumping through hoops, Jayce."

My words, that should have dripped with unapologetic sass, left my lips as a needy purr. In that moment, I was like a cat in heat.

He licked his lips menacingly slow, his eyes never leaving mine.

I parted my lips to take a breath through them.

My nipples strained against the fabric of my dress. His eyes fell to them only for a moment before they rolled up to meet mine again to wink at me.

The elevator's sensor blared, signaling the doors would close without stopping, and I jumped back while he finally removed his foot. Our stares never wavered until the doors closed between us.

———

An hour or so later, my *Uber* pulled up to the back of my mother's residence, my old home, in East Hampton, Long Island. I needed to get my mind right, to receive a reminder as to what the hell I was doing at *Brown, Bloom & Associates* after that moment in the elevator with Jayce. I could've driven my car that was parked in the parking garage a block from my apartment, but I needed to get to my mother's before I did something stupid. If I'd gone straight home, I surely would have used Jayce's number and invited him over to put me out of my misery.

"Summer!" my mother cooed as she pulled opened the back door. "Doll, what are you doing here?"

I stepped into my mother's extended arms and gave her two air kisses on each cheek.

"I thought I'd stop by, tell you all about my first day."

"Yes! Oh, I'm so excited to hear about it." She grabbed my hand, her hands so soft they felt like one million rose petals. "Come, come. Agatha made mimosas. We can sip and talk."

My mother's East Hampton's mansion where I grew up was a little over eight thousand square feet with five bedrooms, six bathrooms, and a pool where I had my first kiss. It also heated up during the cold months. The mansion sat on a 2.3 acre lot and had south facing rooms that bathed in natural light during sunrises and sunsets. I've always loved this home, but not enough to stay after graduating high school. I wanted out from beneath my mother's thumb, but not necessarily out of New York. So *Langston University* was my first choice pick.

My mother and father's brief love affair lasted all but three weeks before they conceived me. But their relationship was long enough for my dad to believe my mother deserved the best. This immense property was one of his tokens of love. He would later marry another woman who my mother claimed is not his true love because she is and always will be.

My mother, Priscilla Baxter, was the quintessential socialite of East Hampton. My father set it up so my mother hasn't had to lift a finger to do so much as file a broken nail. Pampered queen is what she was. I loved that and loved my mother to the moon and back.

"So, talk," she said, her honey brown skin glowing from a recent facial, I'm sure.

I inhaled and released my breath through my mouth.

"So..." I closed one eye and peeked at her through the other. "I was late."

"Summer," she scolded, shaking her head.

"I know, I know." I pressed my fingers to the innermost corners of my eyes, then crossed my arms. "I kicked myself enough about it mother, please don't make me have to do it again."

"Ok, no worries." She lifted her glass to her lips to sip. "I'll call Marie in the morning and will concoct some convincing excuse to explain your tardiness. But no more Summer. I taught you better than that."

"But the train..."

"*Shh, shh*," she shushed. "No more."

I uncrossed my arms.

"Did you lay eyes on any of the associates?" She wiggled her perfectly waxed brows.

"Mother..."

"A career is fabulous doll, especially at your young age. Your father would be so proud. Wait until I tell him where you are interning."

I blushed.

"But... a career won't keep you warm at night. Trust me. I know all about sleeping alone when the man who has your heart is sharing a bed with someone else one state away."

My head tilted to the side when I reached my hand across the table to take hers.

"Oh I'm fine dear." She turned her hand to hold mine. "I just want better for you is all."

I nodded.

"So." She sipped again. "What's the competition like?"

"Oh, mother..." I shook my head.

"That low, huh?" she quizzed.

"The lowest, but, I guess they'll do. They seem bright."

"Hmph."

"There's this one guy, from my school, who I can't figure out."

"What's his family's background?"

One you wouldn't approve of, I'm sure, I thought.

"Not worth mentioning." I lifted my glass of mimosa and brought the rim to my lips.

"Then *he's* not worth mentioning, yes?"

All I did was look her way as I sipped.

"I already conceded to you attending *Langston University*."

"Conceded?" I parroted. "Mother, *LU* is one of the top private universities in the country."

"It's a fabulous school, one of the best, but," she said holding up a finger for emphasis, "it's too *accessible* to people of a certain class and isn't an Ivy League."

I bit my lips closed.

"I say all that to say this... no more talk of this *boy*, okay? No boy who attended that school is good enough for you."

I bounced my head up and down, agreeing.

"Only the best for my only princess."

I smiled.

"Let me get Agatha in here so she can whip us up something delicious to celebrate the first day of your life at *Brown, Bloom & Associates*." She squealed with excitement. "I'm *so* excited, doll, beyond thrilled!"

I laughed as she exited the kitchen. Her long pressed hair bounced in its ponytail as she pranced over white marbled floors to beckon our cook to fire up the stove.

That's right. I'm interning at one of the top law firms in North America. My focus should be on that. Securing a position at the firm would set my life on course in a direction I've always wanted, always dreamed about. Well, not exactly. Getting my name on the directory at *BBA* is what *my mother* always wanted for me once I showed interest in studying law. *She's* always dreamed of me calling that law firm my second home but, hey, same thing... right?

Then why was it that all I could think about, all I could anticipate was seeing Jayce again?

Four

"What up, pops?" I grabbed the rim of my fitted baseball cap to turn it to the back.

The breeze blew through the dried leaves on the grass as I crouched down a bit.

"I told you I'd come to see you the day after I started my internship."

I lowered down into a squat and took a seat on the narrow leaves.

"It's dope so far. I'm competing against seven other people. They look like they're gonna be a lot of competition, but I'm ready. And it's like you always told me, the victory is sweeter when the win doesn't come easy."

My back was against his headstone when I stretched my legs out in front of me.

Carl Martin, my father, died when I was 13-years-old. I can still remember the night my mother woke me from sleep to deliver the news.

"I moved into my new place," I revealed, my eyes fixed ahead of me. "It's in Harlem. A nice little studio spot. I love the neighborhood, it's mad cultured pops. You'd like it. Can't wait till mom and the twins come out and see it. Wish you were here to see it too."

On his way home from work, officers stopped my pops and told him he fit the description of a carjacker who'd hit less than a mile away.

Fit the description.

I scoffed at the thought.

The only description my pops fit was that he was black and seemed young.

Anyway, he was reaching for his ID - something he always advised us never to do whenever police stopped us, whether in a car or on foot - when one officer got trigger happy and shot him in the chest. Paramedics were too late. The officers didn't place the call on time to save his life, too busy trying to figure out a way to cover their asses. My father bled out on the asphalt before help arrived.

"Baby," my mother whispered before entering my room.

My twin brother and sister shared a room with me back then. And we'd continue to share one up until I graduated from LU.

The two of them were sound asleep on their bunk beds when my mother stepped closer to my bed.

My eyes were heavy. I was still groggy, but I noticed my mother's face was wet with tears.

"What's the matter?" I asked her. "Why are you crying?"

"Something happened to your father. I gotta go to the hospital."

I shot up immediately. "What happened to him?"

"He got hurt."

She would never be the one to tell me he was shot and killed. My grandmother did, because my mother had fallen into a deep depressive state soon after seeing my father's body.

The courts never tried the officers involved in the death of my father. The worst they got was desk duty. They were back on the streets a month later.

Not understanding how people, officers at that, could murder someone and get away with it, I got a library card and started borrowing law books from *Brooklyn's Central Library* to study the law. I needed to learn the one thing I believed would keep me and my family breathing, and that could've saved my father. In the process, I fell in love with the idea of being a lawyer to all.

I glanced down at my hands, focusing on the lines that formed an *M* on my palm. Suddenly her face came to mind, her last name at least.

"There's this girl," I said to the air. "Summer McKoy."

I smiled, then laughed at myself for being so corny.

"Pops, I remember you said never to refer to a woman as anything besides a queen, but shorty is for sure a witch with a capital B, yo. For real."

I raised a fist to my mouth to laugh into.

"She is *so* damn stuck up. I don't understand it. She acts like talking to anybody that isn't herself is her doing *us* a favor." I shook my head. "But she is so beautiful... *God* she's gorgeous." I leaned my head against the headstone and stared up at the sky. "She got these eyes that are like a cat's. Real bold with her stare, too. I ain't never seen her smile before, like never, ever. But, I bet when she does, it's sunny, like her name."

My head was leveled when my eyes gazed off into the distance. I ran my hand down the length of my jaw.

"I shouldn't be thinking about that girl right now, anyway. Books before broads right?"

I bobbed my head in a slow up and down motion.

"It's just that... I don't know. Every time I see her, I feel like I gotta shoot my shot. Like maybe this time, I'll crack through this wall she got up."

A smile pulled at my lips.

"And I know she wants me. Well, it's clear now. Yesterday, I saw something in her eyes that was so telling. She looked at me different. It wasn't even a look. She *feasted* her eyes on me like she was hungry and I was her next meal. Shit was sexy, honestly. Summer was the one girl at *LU* I was interested in, but she didn't even glance my way for more than a few seconds." I kissed my teeth. "And I know, *I know* what you're saying right now. You're like, *'son,'*" I said in his voice, *'where's your focus? You need not be chasing any girls, let them come to you,'* right?"

My head bounced up and down. "Yeah, that's what you're saying, but I gotta have her. I'm just unsure if it's only one night I want with her or if this thing is something more."

I bit my lip in thought, my eyes darting from left to right. After a few moments of that, I shook my head and laughed at myself. Summer really had me out here trippin'.

"I found a house for ma and the twins, but ma is so damn stubborn, pops. She *hates* the PJs but don't even want to go to the open house to check out the house because she thinks she can't afford it."

I lifted my cap to scratch the back of my head.

"One of my frat brothers helped me with finding this program for first-time home buyers. If you come with a certain amount for the down payment, they'll loan you the money for the rest of what they're asking for the house. But check it, ma isn't aware that I got about forty-two grand saved in the bank and all I need is 8K more to put down on the house.

You know how I did it? I saved and didn't spend what was left from my scholarship money every semester, created and sold art online from my laptop while using that same laptop to write papers for the team which they paid me for. I'm shaping my house buying plans around the ten thousand dollar sign-on bonus the firm promises to pay out to the intern who wins the position. So, fingers crossed that's me, and my plan actually becomes a reality. I'm banking on it, literally. The family *needs* this win."

I chuckled, knowing I'd gotten my hustler's spirit from my father.

"You should know that I ain't gonna keep playing basketball anymore. You had this dream for me to play in the NBA, but that's not for me. I only played to get through school. I hope you can understand."

I leaned back a bit to pull my phone out my pocket to check the time.

10:16 a.m.

"Anyway, pops, I gotta head back home, shower, get dressed, and make my way to the firm. I have to be there in an hour and a half, and the lawyer we're working under made it clear he isn't playing any games with lateness. He already warned about tardiness."

I turned over on my hands to help me stand up and walked a few feet up from the headstone. I'd learned after my father's burial that they buried people with their feet to the headstones in this cemetery. So, ever since learning that, I've always faced forward with my back to his head-stone and facing him.

"Until next time." I crouched down to the spot that I imagined my father laid, kissed my hand, then pressed my fingers to the blades of grass.

"Be easy, pops. I love you."

FIVE

"Your party?" the hostess asked me at the door. I'd arrived at *GrayArea* restaurant, lounge, & bar twenty minutes after the time our group agreed to meet up.

"Brown, Bloom & Associates," I told her.

"Perfect," she chirped, rolling her greens up from her clipboard to focus on me again. "The rest of your party have already arrived. You can follow me."

She sauntered ahead as my eyes roamed the place. I'd heard of *GrayArea* a few times but never myself stepped foot inside. It was exquisite. Round circular tables, expensive drapes that hung over large window panes. The lighting was exclusively pendant, they resembled heavy earrings for the ceiling. It was a little crowded in there, but not surprising given the day and hour.

Voices murmured around me as the hostess guided me to the table where I saw the top of seven heads.

The interior decorators responsible for *GrayArea's* décor styled the tables in crystal glasses and tiny candles set in intricate votive, the flames dancing with the air in the room.

I arrived at our table and was greeted by seven pairs of eyes that glared up at me. Their faces wore scowls, all except for one... Jayce.

He smiled at me, displaying his perfectly white and shiny rows of teeth.

"So I'm a little late." I pulled out the chair in front of me. "Sue me."

"Allow me to do a little research to verify if that's possible," Veronika said beside Jayce.

I rolled my eyes and placed my bag on the table. The moment I plopped down and into my seat, the diamond tennis bracelet I wore around my right wrist slinked off and fell to the table.

"Shit," I mumbled, snatching up the thin rope of diamonds.

"Cheap things never last," Veronika sassed.

"I agree, they don't," I retorted while clasping the bracelet to my wrist. "This, however, is an 8-carat diamond tennis bracelet from *Tiffany's*. Notice how the flaws in my stones wink at the light." I oscillated my wrist for her to see. "So, what that means, in layman's terms of course, is that I've got your rent for the rest of the year on just my arm tonight."

She scoffed. I smirked.

"The clasp is just old," I added. "I've had it for years. I have to find the time to take it to my jeweler to have it replaced."

"Whatever, look," Carter, the oldest, spoke up at the other end of the table. "We've been here waiting for you to order."

"So, let's order," I replied, glancing his way once the bracelet was back around my wrist.

"You could say *thank you for waiting for me*," Xiomara suggested with a grin.

I grimaced. "Thank you for doing what you all are *expected* to do?! For what? That makes no sense."

Veronika kissed her teeth.

"Guys..." I shrugged. "I'm, what? Twenty minutes late? It's not that big of a deal."

They all groaned. Again, all except for Jayce.

My eyes moved to him. He surprised me by not joining in on the roast. It seemed his speed. I guess if his eyes weren't so busy burying themselves in my cleavage like some type of sand turtle, he would have opened his mouth to speak.

I lifted the menu over my breasts, breaking his focus.

When his eyes met mine, I mouthed, "Nope."

He barked out a laugh that almost made me join in. It intrigued me how he found me dismissing him amusing. Usually people found offense in that, or became combative, but never amused.

"It almost happened again," he said across the table, lifting his menu. "I'm gonna get you to smile by the end of the night, Ms. McKoy."

I raised my menu higher to hide my face and the smile threatening to spread across my lips.

The night progressed. The crew shared information about themselves with each other, their way of getting to know one another. They were boring to me. So boring, I couldn't help my eyes from wandering over to the only interesting person at the table besides me, Jayce. Whenever an intern spoke, my eyes disobeyed my intentions and moved his way. And every time I did that, I noticed his eyes doing the same. It happened so often, I couldn't tell who was initiating glances after a while.

"Anyone here in a relationship?" Veronika asked.

"I'm married," Carter announced.

"So am I," Rolanda confirmed, wiggling her ring finger that held a tiny diamond wedding band. "Two years next week."

"Well, I'm single," Veronika spoke next, her eyes shifting to her right at Jayce. "How about you?"

"Single," he answered, his eyes on me.

David, Morrison, and Xiomara all proclaimed their single status with Morrison announcing he was gay.

"I knew it," I said to him. "My gaydar is top of the line precise and it was sounding the alarm the moment I saw you."

He laughed.

"And how about you, Ms. McKoy," Jayce quizzed ahead of me. The way he said my last name made my walls contract. "What's your marital status?"

"I'm dating... myself," I replied.

He snickered.

"That doesn't surprise me," Veronika spoke up. "You clearly love yourself *a lot*."

"Oh absolutely, and with every fiber of my being." I lifted my glass of water to my lips to sip. "What is there *not* to love *a lot*?"

Jayce and my eyes met again. He folded his bottom lip into his mouth and slowly dragged his teeth over it.

I exhaled a shaky breath through my lips. "I need a drink pronto."

"Yes!" Rolanda shouted. "Now we're talking."

We were all on our second round of drinks when the group had completely loosened up. Predictably, all the ladies either ordered something fruity or wine. I was on my second whiskey sour, when I raised my hand to get the waiter's attention to order a third.

Jayce tilted his glass of cognac in front of his mouth. "I never took you for a whiskey girl, Summer."

I pursed my lips. "What kind of girl did you take me to be then?"

"A wine connoisseur, red. I thought all ladies drank wine."

"Well, not this one," I replied, finishing my drink and raising my hand again for the waiter. Once I captured his attention, I raised my glass and held up one finger.

"You throw those back like a guy," Veronika teased.

"I love my whiskey and my whiskey loves me."

Her usual sass would have gotten on my nerves on any other day, but with my liquor in my system and my head light, she was but a blip in my night.

"For the single people at the table," David said to the right of me. He too was throwing them back so his words were slightly slurred. "What's everyone's type?"

I leaned back in my seat. "Really? Are we *really* about to have that kind of conversation?"

"Well, Summer, we all know that your type is... you," Morrison pointed out with a grin.

I winked. "Naturally."

The table erupted in laughter.

Morrison continued, "But what kind of guys do you like?"

My eyes on their own darted to Jayce before I forced my view off him.

"Refined gentlemen."

"And what's *refined* to you?" Jayce asked.

"No man at this table." I stared ahead of me and right at him.

"Burn!" Xiomara laughed out loud. "Straight no chaser, huh Summer?"

"Just being honest," I answered.

After my refill arrived, I sipped slowly, listening to the others detail their ideal mates. All of them stated attributes unseen to the naked eye. All of this *beauty is within* bullshit.

"I want someone with a good heart," Veronika slurred. She was the second to last to go, Jayce still waiting his turn. "Tall, enchanting eyes, and a deep voice." Her eyes peered over at him as she smiled. "How about you Jayce?"

"I like my women bold," Jayce revealed. "Outspoken with a sharp tongue and jaw-dropping good looks, of course." He held his hands up in supplication. "I might sound shallow, and I apologize, but I gotta be attracted to her, right? Something on her has to be fine. Even if no one else thinks she's fine, she gotta be fine to me."

Everyone at the table snickered.

"I'm a legs and ass man," Jayce continued, "so she got to have that too. But most importantly, a woman who puts up a challenge intrigues me."

My eyes remained on his as I finished the last of my drink. If I knew none better, I'd think he described... me.

"Hmph." Veronika huffed beside him. "That sounds like me."

I snorted, then broke out into a laugh.

"What's so funny?" Veronika sniped.

My laugh had settled into a smile when Jayce and I made eyes with each other. I noticed when he released a long exhale and licked his lips after.

"Not fair." Jayce's eyes were on me, but his head was angled to face Veronika. "I tasked myself with making her mean ass laugh tonight."

The table of interns chuckled, all except Veronika and I.

His focus on me veered down into my cleavage for the umpteenth time that night, but this time I noticed the low-lid stare. He observed me like I was an entrée left off the menu. Like he hadn't had a thing to eat that day.

And that did me in.

Veronika's lips balled as her eyes moved between Jayce and I. She folded her arms and reclined in her seat, conceding to something I never saw coming.

Six

JAYCE

The moment I pushed the door open to step out into the humid summer night, I spotted her standing to the side, tapping along her phone.

It was after midnight. The dinner was a success. All the interns seized the opportunity to get to know each other a little better, and I got a chance to witness Summer with her hair down.

We attended parties together at *LU*. Well, not *together* exactly. She'd be there, and I'd be there too, and often we didn't exchange words, not even *hi*. But I'd never seen her so open the way she was tonight, approachable even. That's probably why I didn't hesitate to walk over to her as she stood outside.

"Need a ride home?" I asked. I buried my hands in my pockets as I focused my eyes down on her.

She angled her chin up at me, exhaled, and focused on her phone again. "*Uber* is telling me a car won't get here for another 15-minutes and I'm ready to hit my bed."

"The night is young." I grinned. "How can you be thinking about sleep right now?"

Summer lifted her gaze to me again and squinted her eyes.

"My boy Damien will be here in the next couple of minutes." I told her. "He drives for *Uber*, but he's not charging, only giving me a lift to Harlem. Where you stay at?"

"West 89th," she answered. "And I doubt *I'll* be getting in your *boy* Damien's car. Thanks, but no thanks."

I shrugged. "Okay." I adjusted the collar of my button down and peeked out into the distance at the flashing red hand at the crosswalk. "It's late and 15-minutes feels more like an eternity when you're standing out in the dark city all alone."

She twisted her mouth to one side.

"And you're tipsy too? Got all that whiskey running through you." I whistled for effect. "But hey... if you're cool with it, it's cool with me."

A black suburban pulled up in front of us and the passenger window rolled down.

Damien tossed his chin up my way from the driver's seat. "What up, Jayce? You ready?"

I lowered my gaze to meet hers. "We ready?"

Her eyes moved to Damien, then back to me. "Well, he doesn't seem sketchy, so... fine."

She walked up ahead of me, my eyes falling to her ass that moved poetically behind her tight red skirt. Summer dressed herself to kill me softly that night. Red cropped top with a distracting v-neck paired with a high-waist, knee-length red skirt that held her tight all over. Her leopard print heels stressed her calves. The muscle stood out a little, hinting at her strength. She had some of the best legs I'd ever seen on a woman her age. I pinched the bridge of my nose when I realized I was staring too damn hard.

She'd arrived in front of the suburban and stepped to the side.

"Are you going to get that?" She pointed at the door.

I chuckled. "Well, of course my lady."

She fought the smile pulling at her lips.

I pulled open the door. "I still need to get you to smile. I ain't forget."

Summer was sliding into the backseat, making room for me to slide in next when she said, "You're going to 278 West 89th Street."

Damien turned in his seat toward her. "Hi, I'm Damien. Oh, me?

I'm fine, thanks for asking, miss strange woman who got in my damn car and didn't say hello."

She rolled her eyes. "I never have to say that much to my previous *Uber* drivers, Damien. Why are you *so* needy?"

My boy's eyes shifted to mine, and I laughed. "Damien, this is Summer. Summer, Damien."

"Summer you are something else." Damien chuckled, facing forward in his seat. "For real."

He pulled out of the parking space and we were on our way.

She glanced over at me to find my attention on her. "What?"

I smiled big. The goal was to disarm her. I noticed every time I smiled at her, her face changed from hard to soft. Her chest rose and fell faster, and she took deeper breaths when I flashed my pearly whites. I needed for her to let her guard down that same way tonight.

I tapped her at the side of her thigh, and her eyes dropped there.

"Yo, what's your deal?"

Her eyes returned on mine.

"Why are you so stuck up and mean?"

"Stuck up and mean?!"

Damien snickered from the front seat.

"Yeah, stuck up and mean," I repeated. "You act like you're better than everybody."

She shrugged. "It's not an act. I am better than everybody."

Damien whistled.

She kissed her teeth. "Can you cool it with the ad-libs up there?"

"Oh, she feisty, feisty," Damien teased. "Yeah, that's your type."

"Who's *type*?" she asked.

"Your man back there with you."

She scoffed, crossing her legs and leaning away from me. "He is *not* my man. The nerve."

"Yet," Damien added.

"Anyway." I scooted closer, draping my arm over the back of her seat. "Why are you so cold?"

"So, because I don't fawn over you like half the female population, I'm cold?"

I folded my bottom lip into my mouth, and she licked hers, forcing her eyes off mine.

"Nah, not exactly."

"If I knew this ride would be a backseat interrogation," she began, "I would've waited the extra ten minutes for my *Uber* to arrive."

"But then you wouldn't be getting first class door-to-door service like this," Damien chimed in. "Or good company like what you're getting with your man Jayce back there."

She kissed her teeth. "You're an excellent wingman, Damien. Top shelf."

"It's a gift," he teased.

Summer giggled. For the second time that night, I watched laugh lines frame her lips. They were subtle. But nothing compared to the two tiny dimples in her cheeks I never noticed before.

"That makes two people tonight that have made you laugh."

Summer pointed her eyes on me.

"You really don't like me, huh?"

We held our stares for a moment. And then she did something I never thought she'd do... she looked away shyly to hide her smile.

"278 West 89th," Damien announced from the front seat.

A frown weighed my lips down instantly. I was a little disappointed that Damien got us there so fast.

Summer lifted her bag and dipped her hand in her purse, pulling out her designer wallet.

"Nah, nah." I held my hand up. "This one is on me."

"I can at least give him a tip."

"Yeah, Jayce." Damien turned in his seat. "She can at least do that."

Summer laughed this time, singling out a fifty-dollar bill from the cash compartment of her *LV* wallet.

She handed it to Damien when he accepted it and smiled with all his teeth. "Yo, Summer! Yeah, shorty, you the one. That's what the fuck I'm talkin' bout ma, whew!"

"Man, hush," I said to Damien, kicking his seat from the back.

"Have a good night gentlemen." She pushed open her door and stepped out. "Bye, Jayce."

Before I could respond, she closed the door.

She lived on a quiet city block in a sandstone brownstone. It was nice and seemed expensive, *really* expensive.

I slapped the back of his headrest. "Yo, D, why you ain't drive slower, man?"

Damien laughed, turning the steering wheel in preparation to pull out of parking.

"Nah, hold up," I told him. "Wait until she goes inside."

"You right, you right."

As soon as she disappeared inside, closing the brownstone's door, Damien pulled out of the spot and we were on our way.

"You wanna do more than smash that one."

"Huh?!"

"Don't *huh* me," Damien replied, glancing at me through his rearview mirror. "I've seen you with the others. You move different with this girl. Engaging in convo, wanting to make sure she walked inside so you know she's safe. This one got your tongue all the way hanging out."

I leaned back in my seat and folded my arms. "Man, whatever."

Something shined in my peripheral the second my shoulders touched the back of the seat. When I glanced that way, then dropped my view to the spot where she sat, I noticed something sparkling on the leather seat. The moment I picked it up, I recognized it as the diamond bracelet she wore earlier in the night.

"She dropped her bracelet."

"Summer?"

"Yeah." I held her bracelet up. The diamonds flickered against the shine of the streetlights as Damien drove past them. "I gotta take it back to her.

"Aren't you going to see her on Monday?"

"Yeah, but..." I licked my lips. "Just circle around the block and let me bring it to her."

"Yo, J, you my boy and all, but it's a busy night. I gotta make this bread before the surge goes away."

"No doubt, I feel you." I tapped his headrest this time. "Aight, so drop me off and I'll find my way home."

"You sure?"

"Yeah." I smirked. "One thousand percent sure."

SEVEN

SUMMER

"I just couldn't text you tonight. It's been so long since I've heard your voice, bestie," Kasha whined on the other end of my phone. I answered the call on speaker so I could continue getting ready for bed.

"Too long," I replied. "So, how's the internship?"

"Already a drag," she groaned. "I've gained at least five pounds eating these damn Philly cheesesteaks. They are so good by the way! Not to mention there isn't one guy here I'd like to fuck to burn some of these damn calories off. You know sex is my cardio."

I snorted a laugh as I stood over my vanity table with one foot perched at the edge of the chair. In my palm, I warmed whipped cocoa butter in my hands, then smoothed the buttery oil down the length of my leg.

"I just got in from the welcome dinner for mine."

"Shut up!" she yelled. "They hosted a welcome dinner for you guys?"

"More like sponsored. None of the partners attended. They just paid for it."

"Still better than what they gave us; stale bagels and lukewarm coffee in a hot ass room. But enough about that..." She cooed, and I already knew why. "How's working with sexy Jayce?"

Like torture is what I wanted to say. But instead I told her, "Annoying."

A cold shower was just what I needed to get my mind right. Being in Jayce's presence was so effecting. What was it about him that made me get like this? His looks? His voice? Or just... *him*?

Kasha giggled. "Looks like both of our internships are a bust. I have no fine guys at mine and you have to work with the one fine ass guy you've hated since your freshman year. But I'd be more than willing to trade places with you."

"*Ugh*," I groaned to myself as I slid my hand down my thigh one final time before twisting the lid closed on my jar of body butter. "I don't think I'm desperate enough to intern at *Kaplan & Gold*, sorry."

"Oh, fuck you, Summer!" Kasha laughed, and I joined in. "We should've backpacked through Europe after graduation like Moni. I saw on her Instagram that she's in Greece this week, next week she's in Italy."

"Ooh, jealous!" I pouted. "I hope she brings me back a souvenir. She better bring me back something."

I slipped on a white tank and a pair of black varsity shorts with a white corded side.

"Anyway, I need to get some shut eye to keep the bags away." I announced. "Talk or text soon?"

"I'll sure try," she answered. "But no promises."

I laughed. "Same, sis, same."

After ending the call with Kasha, I fell into my vanity's chair and reached for the makeup remover wipes beside my crystal glass jar of makeup brushes.

You should have removed your makeup before your shower, doll.

I could hear my mother chastising me in my head per usual.

If you shower first, the steam from the water will open your pores, foundation will seep into them, clog them, and you will wake up with hideous pimples by the morning.

I chuckled as I peeled apart the wipes.

The moment I moved on campus, it thrilled me to be out of the Hampton's mansion. I loved my mother, sincerely I did, but my goodness did she scrutinize every little thing that pertained to me.

My eyes wandered up to the mirror to remove my earrings. Instinctively, my eyes dropped to my wrist to unclasp my diamond tennis bracelet next. The brows over my eyes shot up when I noticed the area bare. I twisted my wrist from left to right as if that would make the bracelet reappear.

My hand flew up to my mouth to cover and my head moved from left to right, examining the surrounding area.

"No!" I cried out. "Shit, I should have taken it off when I got in."

Up and out of my seat, I headed straight for the bathroom since I was there last. When I didn't find it in there, I searched around the other areas of my apartment for anything long and shimmery.

"That damn clasp," I mumbled to myself. "Where the hell is my bracelet?!"

My diamond tennis bracelet was more than a bracelet to me though.

I immediately retraced my steps, walking to the front door and then reentering the living space.

My apartment was small. Housed in a Manhattan brownstone, a studio-like living habitat was where I called home. Mother had the rent paid in full up until next summer.

The bedroom and living room shared the same space divided by a white sheer curtain draped inches in front of my bed, so there wasn't much space to search. My place was tiny, so where was it?!

Suddenly, my phone chirped on my vanity, but I ignored it to keep looking.

My father gifted me that tennis bracelet for my 18th birthday. Well, actually, my mother handed me the wrapped box it was in, but she insisted my father bought the bracelet himself.

The phone rang once more, so I snatched it up and off my vanity table, peeked down at the name sprawled along my screen, and wrinkled my nose.

"This better be important," I spat when I answered the call. "I'm in the middle of looking for something."

"Your bracelet?"

"Yes, actually. How'd you know—"

"I have it." His bass-filled voice was like food for my ear. I paused my search when a shiver ran down my back causing me to shake. "You dropped your bracelet in the backseat of Damien's car."

I gasped. "You have it?!"

"I do."

"Oh my God, thank God!"

"I'm in front of your place," he made known next. "Do you want to come down and get it?"

"Just come up. I'm not at all dressed to fetch anything." I approached the built-in intercom system beside my door. "Pull the door. I'm buzzing it opened."

He hung up after that. A minute or two later, I heard a knock at my door.

When I opened it, I saw my bracelet coiled around his index finger.

"Yes!" I held my hand out for it. "I thought I'd lost it. Was looking all over..."

My words trailed off when I noticed where his eyes had fallen. His roaming orbs focused on everything except for my eyes. First, they started their journey down my neck and around my breasts. His visual tour of me continued past my waist to my hips, then lingered at my legs.

The more he stared, the hotter I got. I waited for the urge to close the door to arrive, but it never surfaced. Instead, I allowed his gawk to continue.

Why was I allowing it to continue?

I cleared my throat to get his attention, and he rolled his eyes up to meet mine.

"Is that all?" I sassed.

Jayce's lips slid slow against his teeth, revealing a smile. I swear Jayce cast a spell on me each time he smiled. He had the most dangerous grin that had enough power to mess with my thinking. I avoided him and that smile for years. An easy thing to do because I never spent more than a few seconds in his company. Now, with the prospect of seeing him five days out of the week during our internship, it was going to be torture.

"*Is* that all?" he asked me.

I swallowed hard, then shut my eyes tight before reopening them.

Jayce lifted his arm and leaned it against the panel of my door. His movements, paired with the draft moving through the hall, brought his scent up my nose. That was the end and the beginning.

"You know..." He licked his lips, moving closer. "If you want me to come in, I can too."

I stared at him.

"All you ever have to do is ask, Ms. McKoy."

There was no way I'd be able to focus with him around. Not just here. Anywhere I was. I had a goal; secure the only available position at the firm that would be offered to only one intern, me. My dad would surely be proud of that. I knew my mother would be.

So, I figured, let me just sleep with Jayce, get it out of my system, and move on with life so I could refocus. Chances are, I was totally romanticizing this guy, allowing my fantasies to overshadow my reality. After-all, it's just sex...

How good in bed could he be, anyway?

My feet were moving before I had enough sense to stop them. I grabbed the hem of his button-down shirt and used it to draw me closer to him. In front of Jayce, a foot below him, he dropped his view to me, his eyes glued to mine.

I balanced myself on the arch of my feet, lifting my lips to his.

On them I whispered, "Come. In."

He crushed his mouth against mine just that fast, held me in place by wrapping his arm around me and pressing his palm to my lower back.

He walked me in my apartment and closed the door with his other hand. Turned with me and pushed me back against the door's surface. His tongue slid into my mouth, and I welcomed it with mine.

I couldn't believe the moan he tongued out of me. And he loved it. I could tell he loved it from the smiling he did on my lips before he pulled away. Jayce lifted the bracelet up to my view and I snatched it out his hand, tossing it on the table near my door and beside my apartment's keys.

His hands cupped my breasts as his mouth returned to mine. His hands were everywhere actually and everywhere he touched I melted even more.

I traced the muscles in his arms with my fingertips as he pinned me against that wooden door, having his way with my mouth. My body was on fire, well past normal body temperature I'm sure. I was so sensitive, every part of me throbbed.

Jayce's hands slid down my waist to my ass where he cupped it in his palms, gave each mound a gentle squeeze, then used my cheeks to lift me up and off my feet, his mouth still on mine.

He wrapped my legs around his waist and carried me through my apartment, found my bed, and dropped me on it.

I raised my gaze to meet his. He unbuttoned his shirt, all the while examining me. His eyes analyzed everything from my hair to my red painted toe nails.

"What are you waiting for to get undressed?"

His words came out as a growl that had the power to make me climax on sight.

Still, I couldn't show how spellbound he held me. "You take it off."

He paused, unbuttoning his shirt to lean toward me on the bed. Jayce balanced himself on his fists, caging me in at my hips. The weight of him against my mattress almost slid me closer to him.

In my face he said, "Summer, if I have to take off any of your clothes, I'm ripping each item off you."

My jaw dropped.

"Yeah." He stood upright to slide his shirt down his arms and off of him.

Breathing became an afterthought the second I laid eyes on his naked torso. God built that man for battle. His physique was that of a fucking warrior. How on earth was that possible?

Jayce resembled one of those Grecian statues my girl Moni was probably photographing right now in Greece. Muscles defined, chiseled even. His biceps were bulbous, his pecs rounded and well-defined. His stomach easily shaped into a neat, portrait-worthy six-pack.

I was in so much trouble and that became abundantly clear as he stood in front of me.

Jayce released his belt, then unbuttoned his slacks.

"You enjoy watching, huh?"

My eyes rolled up to meet his to find a smirk on his lips.

I smirked back. "The queen often likes when her jesters entertain."

He laughed from his gut, and when his amusement faded, a cocky grin remained on his lips.

Speaking of cocky...

Jayce pulled his pants down, followed by his boxers. I couldn't stop my smirk from morphing into a dropped jaw or my eyes from bulging out. The man was heavily hung. Emphasis on heavy. It looked unreal. Online adult toy shop unreal.

"Oh, shit," I exhaled then swallowed hard.

"Mm-hmm. Tonight," he declared, climbing atop my bed and headed straight for me. "I'm gonna humble you."

He pounced on top of me, taking my breath away.

Jayce didn't rip my clothes off exactly, although I'm sure he came close to doing it. He pulled my shirt overhead and damn near tore my shorts as he snatched them off. Turned me over onto my stomach and used his teeth to peel my panties off me last.

Between the whiskey flowing through my veins, the smell of our natural scents mingling in the air, I thought I'd pass out from antic-ipation.

Breathe, Summer. Breathe.

He licked me from the back of my calves up to the apex of my thighs. Buried his mouth between my cheeks before he slid his tongue to my clit.

Jayce sucked on my pink nub from behind me. He had me circling my hips and pushing my pussy against his mouth like an eager amateur. I was practically begging for his next lick. Whimpering. Moaning with angst. And when the stir of my orgasm suddenly arrived with no warn-ing, and way too soon if you ask me, I stretched my hand behind me to hold his head in place so he'd keep flitting his tongue around and around on that one spot. And he allowed it, allowed me to ride his face until my climax faded, never breaking momentum until he sensed I was done.

Jayce used my legs to turn me over and onto my back. In the middle of catching my breath, I watched him rip open a condom with his teeth, tossing the wrapper behind him and sliding the *Magnum XL* down his very hard erection.

He crawled on the bed to me and brought his lips to mine. I tasted me on his tongue, inhaled my release on his facial hair. Felt him scoop me up, then carry me to the head of my bed as if I weighed nothing.

Jayce laid me there then reached down between us, with no pause, guiding himself in.

My mouth hung open in response to the sweet ache from the accommodating stretch of my walls. No sound came out of me as he buried his bone in me.

He planked overhead, watching me the whole time, his bottom lip in a vice between his top and bottom teeth.

And when he started thrusting in and out, I lost it, completely. I couldn't shut the fuck up.

"You ain't loud enough though," he taunted in my ear as his pace quickened.

His pelvis crashed into me, and I did my best to meet each stroke. I laid my hand against his ass, feeling his gluteal muscles contract and release each time he fed me his hard-on.

"Oh my *God, oh* my God!"

Jayce parted my lips with his and dipped his tongue into my mouth, his lingual movements matching the deep strokes he delivered between my thighs.

"I knew your pussy was good," he whispered against me.

Not a moment later, he pulled out of me and used my hip to turn me over on my stomach again. His hands gripped the creases where my hips and thighs met, using them to lift me to my knees.

Jayce was merciless when he slid in me again and took me from behind. I was mumbling indiscernible things that even I couldn't make out. His grunts and growls were truly sending me.

Sweat perfumed the air and glossed our figures. Our bodies were covered in so much perspiration, our pelvis's joining sounded like the applause of wet palms.

His hand combed through my hair before he held a fistful of it and pulled, using my strands as reins of sorts to pull me on to him so he could go deeper make me feel every bit of him, not allowing even an inch to go to waste.

A coiling feeling in my belly grabbed my attention first, then the pulsing of my walls soon after. I felt heavy all over, but light in my core as my body vibrated on him.

"Yeah, Summer, come for me baby."

I met his crashes, slamming back against him, my teeth bared, eyes slowly rolling to the back of my skull.

The shaking my lower body did could not be controlled. Jayce returned his hands to my thighs' creases and helped me to keep up with his strokes. The man was a damn athlete on the courts and in bed. He kept rhythm, inhaling and exhaling through his mouth while never skipping a breath. I just couldn't keep up with him or hold out any longer.

My orgasm crashed into me and made my legs give out, causing me to fall face first against my pillow. Jayce planted his arms on either side of me and continued to drill in and out, never losing his rhythm, as I trembled with no restraint below him. My moans were so loud they echoed in the space around us.

He pressed his lips to my hair and roared his release into the nape of my neck. I bit my pillow to muffle my moans as he shuddered atop me, his strokes slowly faltering to a stop.

For a few moments, we caught our breaths together, as one still connected down below. He eventually rolled off and onto his back and I did the same, our chests rising and falling beside one another.

So, I was right to question his bed skills and if he was any good, because he wasn't *good*. He was great. The best.

Shit.

"Damn, Jayce," I whispered at the ceiling, not even meeting my eyes with his. "Wow!"

When I finally turned my head to him, I found a king-sized smile on his lips. "Wow, yourself."

Still breathing hard, he sat up briefly to grab his trousers, dipped his hand into his pocket and pulled out a handful of gold-wrapped condoms, tossing them on my night table.

My eyes ballooned at the sight.

"You all rested up?" he asked, pulling off the condom he wore and dropping it in my waste basket at my bedside. "Because that was just the warm up."

My jaw hinged opened. "Wh-what? The warm up?!"

Jayce chuckled, grabbing another condom from the pile on my night table, bringing the wrapper to his lips and ripping it open with his teeth. He nodded his answer as he slid the condom down his dick that was still very erect. "If you haven't realized yet... you in trouble with me. There will be no sleeping tonight, princess."

"Fuck," I whispered right before he pounced on me.

He grabbed my wrists and pinned them over my head with one hand.

"Oh, I intend to," he growled as he reached down between us with the other. "And I plan to fuck all night, Ms. McKoy." Jayce smirked while sliding in slowly, groaning his return inside me. I exhaled as he inched in, only stopping when I was full of him yet again. On my lips he whispered, "Round two."

EIGHT

Her eyes were the first things I saw when I slid opened the conference room door. Summer warmed the seat in her usual spot at the head of the table. She followed me with her eyes, a smile teeming on her lips.

I chuckled at the sight.

"Good morning, y'all," I greeted, pulling out my chair. My fingers were at the button of my gray Calvin Klein slim fit suit jacket when I locked my eyes on hers. "How was everybody's weekend?"

As the room of interns chimed in about what they did or didn't do, I watched Summer tuck her lips in her mouth and bite them closed, trying her damndest to bite back her smile.

I knew exactly how her weekend was. She spent all of it with me... with me on her and her on me.

"How about you, Summer?" I quizzed, leaning back in my chair, stroking my goatee once I found comfort in my seat.

She pressed the tip of her tongue against the inside of her cheek.

I licked my lips. "How was your weekend?"

Summer had a lot of mouth, and attitude, but in bed? In bed I discovered she was all woman. Gone was that sharp tongue and slick mouth of hers. I made sure to make her submit to me in ways that shocked even her, leaving her no choice but to acknowledge the power I wielded. From Friday night into Saturday morning and then again that Saturday afternoon, I worked her over to the point of exhaustion. She couldn't even walk right to see me off at her door. I left her sated. And I couldn't lie... I wanted an encore of that show.

"My weekend was very... *satisfying*," she replied. Summer lifted her paper cup of coffee to her lips and gulped what remained in it.

I couldn't help the chuckle that left my lips.

"Oh, good," Jeff said at the door. "Everyone is early which means you are on time."

He walked in with Stephanie on his heels. She slid the door closed as soon as they were both inside.

"Good morning *BBA* warriors." He grinned. "You my magnificent eight will get your first assignment today. Lucky you."

He ran his hand down his salt and pepper beard, then pointed his chin at Stephanie who turned to hit the light switch.

Less than a second later, Jeff switched on the overhead projector at the back of the room, and ahead on the projector's screen appeared a picture of a beautiful black woman. She had short hair and a wide, radiant smile. She was thinner than I like but still a woman who could make any man do a double take.

"This is our new client, Melissa Hatchett."

We all focused on the screen.

"Steph," he called, "Take it away."

"Melissa," Stephanie began, "would have married her fiancé, Timothy Warren, last spring, but he was gunned-down by an off-duty officer three hours before his wedding."

The muscles in my stomach tightened.

"A year later, the officer involved in the shooting is now dead and his blood is on her hands."

"How'd that happen?" Xiomara asked.

"Melissa here," Jeff chimed in, "carried on an affair with Adan Esposito, the slain officer, and killed him in his sleep two months ago."

"Do we know what led to her fiancé's death?" I asked. "Why the officer shot him?"

"Minor traffic incident," Stephanie answered. "Her fiancé supposedly changed lanes inappropriately, and Officer Esposito, pulled him over for it. According to the incident report, as Officer Esposito approached the vehicle to address Timothy, he noticed Timothy reach into his glove compartment and pull out something black and shiny. Convinced it was a gun, the officer fired his service weapon, killing Timothy at the scene."

"What was Timothy retrieving from the glove compartment?" Summer asked.

Jeff inhaled sharply. "His registration jacket. Melissa believes he was reaching for the information to make the stop a quick one since he was already late arriving at the hotel to get dressed for the wedding."

I shook my head. This was eerily familiar to me, being the child of a man murdered at the hands of police.

Stephanie switched on the lights.

"As you have already predicted," Jeff continued, "this case won't be an easy one. Reasonable doubt is what the goal is. We're dealing with the death of an officer at the hands of a woman who was engaged to the man *that* officer killed. Already the prosecution have their sights on premeditated murder, which is not of a benefit to us. The judge will want to throw the book at Melissa just to make an example out of her."

"Not to mention," I started, "the officers at the precinct where Officer Esposito worked will have nothing but great things to say about him." I clenched my teeth just thinking back to a similar scenario after officers murdered my father. The officers who did it were supposedly the best in the unit with no issues before taking my father's life... if you let their captain tell it.

Jeff's eyes lowered to mine. "You're right. And I know you know that from experience."

I drew in a deep breath.

"Will you be okay working on this case? Is it a trigger?"

Without thought, my eyes rolled over to Summer's to see the space between her brows puckered.

"Although my father was murdered by a cop years ago, I can work on this. It isn't a trigger." I made eye contact with Jeff again. "I'm good."

I shifted my view on Summer for only a moment to see a frown weighing her lips down before she mouthed, "I'm so sorry."

I bowed my head in response then looked up at Jeff.

"All right then," he continued. "Now, as I've told you all on your first day – this internship is not about making copies and getting me coffee. You're here to be courtroom assistants and part of that is preparing for our days in court and in front of a jury. I need you guys to work in teams. So, choose your partners now, and wisely, so Stephanie can make a note of it."

Summer and I glanced at each other again. We both parted our lips to say something when Veronika spoke first.

"Jayce and I can partner up." Veronika smiled and winked at me.

"Uh..." I began. I focused on Summer again, thinking she would chime in but all she did was scoff and roll her eyes while leaning back in her seat.

My head tilted to the right at her reaction. She was jealous.

"Okay," I said to Veronika. "Sure."

Truthfully, I had to keep my head in the game and my eye on that 10K. I had a lot riding on getting that sign-on bonus, and Summer would no doubt be a distraction from that as a partner.

Speaking of Summer, the moment I agreed to team up with Veronika, Summer blinked her eyes away from mine and shook her head.

"Want to team up, Summer?" Xiomara asked to her left.

"Yeah, sure," Summer spat. "Whatever."

The room continued to buzz with chatter until all the interns partnered up.

"That was quick," Jeff complimented. "I like that a lot. Continue to impress me. Your first team assignment is researching past litigations that are similar in nature and drafting up questions you believe will be useful for our cross examination. I want all of you to drum up at least ten questions a piece. Review the case with a keen eye. Each team will receive their own file. Once you are familiar with everything and I do mean *everything*, draft your inquiries. Get them over to Stephanie by the end of the week and she will give you your next assignment. Everyone got it?"

The room offered a resounding, "Yes."

When I glanced over at Summer, I saw her rubbing her lips together,

her eyes locked on mine. I tossed my chin up at her and she shifted her eyes away.

———

A few hours later and with a growling stomach, I stepped out of the office to find something to eat. It was around one in the afternoon, and the sidewalks were bustling with the lunch hour crowd. Most in suits like myself or in construction uniforms taking a break from working on the several buildings that were being built or renovated around midtown.

I stopped at a burger joint a few blocks south of the office. Grabbed myself a bacon and cheese grilled sirloin on a pretzel bun with fries and walked my way back to the office building with plans to eat upstairs with the other interns. I was across the street when I noticed her legs and that ass. They were easy to recognize because I'd seen them in rare form over the weekend. Those legs wrapped around my waist, that ass up in the air. My dick twitched just thinking about her flexibility.

Summer wore her usual pencil skirt and a blazer, with a simple blouse that showed her cleavage underneath. Today, the skirt and blazer were black while her top an innocent powder pink. She held a plastic container of green salad in one hand as she scrolled down her phone's screen with the other.

A homeless guy dressed in a tattered black t-shirt, soiled ripped jeans, and severely stained tennis sneakers approached her with a paper cup in hand extended.

"Hmph," I huffed, sure of how the scene would play out, knowing her at least.

Instead of Summer cringing or shooing the homeless guy away, she did the opposite. Without hesitation, Summer reached into her purse and pulled out her wallet, singling out two bills, folding and placing the money in his cup.

"Hmm," I hummed this time. "Interesting."

He thanked her repeatedly as he walked away, and she gave him a closed-mouth smile before her eyes focused on the screen of her phone again.

Definitely wasn't expecting that, I thought to myself as I made my way across the street.

I was close when I asked, "Are you going back up right now?"

She moved her eyes off her phone and lifted them up to mine before doing a double take. Summer slid her device into her purse, then scanned her eyes around me. "I thought for sure you'd be eating with your new *partner*."

I smirked. "Nah, I needed a bit of a break from Roni."

"*Roni*?" The right side of her lip curled up in disgust. "*Ugh*."

I snickered. "You know..." I moved in closer. "If you would have spoken up, I probably would have told her thanks but no thanks and partnered with you. Now we'll never know."

"I don't chase," she stated. "That's how the crown tilts."

I licked my lips slow. Her slanted baby doll cat eyes peered into mine. Instantly I remembered how they looked rolling to the back of her head and how her mouth hung open as they did.

She must have noticed my gawk because she cleared her throat a second later then ran her palm down the back of her head.

"Besides," she added, "it's clear Veronika, or as you call her *Roni*, has it bad for you and I'm not in the mood to step on toes."

I smiled, and she glanced away.

"Roni's cool but," I replied, moving in, "I can't seem to get you off my mind."

She stared at me.

"Or off my lips."

Summer slid the tip of her tongue along her top teeth. "Tough."

I glanced around us to check for familiar faces. When I'd seen no one we knew, I moved in even closer and leaned in, grazing my lips against the shell of her ear.

I said low, "Do you know I can still taste your pussy on my tongue?"

She gasped, then gently pushed me back. The biggest smile I'd ever seen her wear spread across her lips and my heart melted. It fucking melted!

Damn this girl.

"Behave," she whispered, puffing air into her shirt.

"At least I made you smile."

Summer scrubbed her fingertips against her brows as she giggled low. Her eyes fell to the bag in my hand.

"A burger and fries?" she uttered. "You will be sleepy before end of day. And the grease... yuck."

"What?" I asked, peeling open the bag and dipping my hand in for a fry. To my lips, I drew the fry in using only my tongue. "I got good taste."

She snorted a laugh. "Yeah, sure."

"I know a lot of fancy places to eat."

"Doubt that," she replied, turning for the turnstile doors.

"I can take you to a few sometime."

She glanced at me over her shoulder. "I'm not stepping on toes, Jayce, remember?"

"But you had me first... several times and in several positions." I grinned.

"*Shh*." She pressed her finger to her heart-shaped lips, then smiled as she pushed through the rotating doors to enter the building.

I blew air out my mouth, watching through the glass as her ass rose and fell with her walk.

"Focus Jayce, focus," I told myself as I entered the building behind her.

NINE

A week and three days after we received our first assignments, myself and the rest of the interns had finally made a little home at *Brown, Bloom & Associates*. We'd gotten acclimated with each other's personalities and everyone was falling in line. I knew the job was mine, my mother secured that, but I still needed to play sort of nice with the others, you know... for the optics a.k.a. the firm's partners.

According to my mother, the lawyers played politics in this place. Any foul attitude can be a turnoff and they talked to each other, so bad news about me would travel fast in this large building.

Brown, Bloom & Associates took up several floors in the building. They specialized in a few areas of law, three of which being business law, entertainment law, and of course where I interned criminal law.

It was a late Thursday afternoon, just an hour before it was time to leave. I'd swallowed down two cups of coffee earlier in the day, and my heavy eyes hinted I would need a third before my workday ended.

I'd entered the break room and found Jayce at the counter, pouring himself a cup of water. He glanced up and kept his eyes on me when I walked in.

We'd perfected the art of keeping things under the radar. We didn't speak much while at the office.

Granted, since that Friday night in my apartment, Jayce and I hadn't hooked up. But I'd be lying if I said I didn't think about doing it again, and soon.

"Another round?" he asked. Jayce leaned against the counter facing me.

Though we hadn't hooked up since that night, he never failed to get the fire going in me with his salacious remarks that seemed innocent to outsiders but always made me want to change panties in the middle of the day.

"I need it," I replied.

"You still haven't called me for that other thing I know you need, too."

"Jayce," I whispered. "Quit."

In his presence, I couldn't prevent the smile that often threatened to curl the corners of my lips up. I was fighting hard not to get smitten with him, get lost in his charm. My mother would kill me if I did.

"Summer, right?" I heard to my right. When I turned in that direction, I locked eyes with a tall and dark gentleman. He had motherland features and skin the color of vanilla, the extract. So highly melanated. His teeth contrasted with his skin tone to create a delicious treat for the eyes.

Yum.

He was tall, maybe a few inches shorter than Jayce. He wore a tailored suit, the inseams fitted to his frame. Short cropped hair, full lips, and broad shoulders completed the visuals.

"That's me," I replied.

"I'm not interrupting anything..." His eyes moved past me to Jayce. "... am I?"

I turned to glance at Jayce over my shoulder, then faced forward again. "No, you're not interrupting anything at all."

"Perfect." He smiled. "Do you have a moment to spare?"

"I should," I answered, turning to pick up my cup of coffee. Jayce and my eyes met, and he stared into me until I broke eye contact with him.

"Great." The gentleman gestured his arm out of the break room. "Let's speak outside."

I nodded, then made my way there, being sure not to twist my neck in Jayce's direction.

We walked along the office's walkway, the brown carpet tiles below us muffling the clicks of our shoes. "I'm Anton. Anton Jacobs."

"It's a pleasure to meet you, Anton."

"Let's rendezvous in my office... if you don't mind."

"You have an office?"

He smiled. "I'm a junior partner here."

Slot machines went off in my head. I'd hit the jackpot without even trying.

The one thing my mother bragged about while handing me the application to apply for my summer internship were the men who worked at *Brown, Bloom & Associates*. They were handsome, well-educated, and paid. She knew for sure I'd find one here to settle down with.

Though I didn't share my mother's enthusiasm for being wedded, bedded, and impregnated, sampling a little eye candy with money couldn't hurt.

Only the best for my only princess, I imagined my mother saying right now.

"Have a seat." He gestured to the chair opposite his desk.

His office was modest, not as immense as Jeff's office or the other partners, but it was better than a shared conference room and none-theless nice. A sizable wooden desk, designer leather chair, and a cute view of the city. Anton was doing all right for himself.

"How's your time here at *BBA* thus far?"

"Rewarding, obviously," I purred.

He chuckled lightly, and I licked my lips.

"Anton, can I be frank?"

He nodded slow.

"You and I both know you did not call me in here to ask me about my time here at the firm, so how about we skip the formalities so I can get back in that room and compete like a big girl."

"I like your sass," he whispered.

"That's what I hear from most." I sipped my coffee.

"Have dinner with me this weekend," he said. "This Saturday."

Forward, good, I preferred forward.

I tilted my head to one side and twisted my lips to the other, giving off the impression I was thinking. This was a move my mother taught me. She always told me never to be too eager. Make them sweat a little so they know how much of a privilege having access to me was. That way they have no choice but to respect me because *I* respect me.

"Where?" I asked.

"Anywhere you'd like."

"Well..." I sipped my coffee again. "*You're* asking me out. So I'd like for *you* to finalize the plans, Mr. Jacobs."

"Noted." His smile grew wider. "So, is that a yes?"

"It's a hell yes," I replied with a wink.

———

"Hi mother!" I squealed into the phone. "Are you busy?"

I forced myself to wait until I was between the four walls of my studio apartment to call my mother. Fought myself not to dial her up seconds after walking out of Anton's office. But as she always said, patience is a virtue.

"I'm never too busy for you, doll," she sang into the phone. "Allison's here giving me my weekly mani and pedi, but my earpiece is in so I am all yours."

"I got asked out on a date." I peeled off my heels and walked them to my walk-in closet.

"By?"

"A junior partner at *BBA*."

My mother gasped. I giggled in response.

"Summer, that is marvelous news, doll! Just marvelous! Oooh! Your father will be so proud to hear you've found someone at the firm."

I cheesed from ear to ear. I'd been hearing about how much my father loved *Brown, Bloom & Associates* since I was a kid. An attorney there represented his portfolio of businesses. He'd never said that to me, but he and my mother talked more than he and I did, apparently.

"So, when is the special day?" she asked.

"This Saturday."

"Perfect. I will be there Saturday morning so we can do some quick shopping. I'll help you choose something stunning for the night."

This wasn't out of the norm. My mother shopping with me or more so shopping *for me* was the usual. She loved to dress me up more than she enjoyed styling the porcelain dolls she kept in her girl cave in the mansion's basement. I was her own little life-sized doll. I appreciated it most days.

"Okay, sounds good to me."

My phone beeping made me pull the device off my ear to see a call coming in.

It was Jayce.

"Uh, mother, I have to... umm... go and get settled in. I called you as soon as I got in so I still need to shower."

"Remember to remove your makeup first, doll," she scolded. "I beg of you. Please do not show up at your date with a pimple you can prevent right now. Clean your face then shower."

"Okay mother." I rolled my eyes.

"Promise me."

"Promise."

She blew a kiss through the phone and I reciprocated before clicking over to Jayce.

"And you're calling me why?"

"I'm downstairs."

The walls inside me contracted and my legs became weak. I couldn't decide if it was his voice that did it or him being just past my door and down some stairs that put me in a state.

"Okay...?" I tried to gather my breath to prevent myself from breathing hard into the phone. "And who told you, you were welcomed to stop by whenever you so chose to?"

He chuckled. "So, do you want me to leave?"

I bit the side of my lip. Of course I didn't, but I had no plans of telling him.

So I walked to my intercom system and buzzed him in.

"Thank you," he voiced, ending the call immediately after.

I remained at the door, sneaking a quick glance at myself in the floor-length mirror at the side of my door.

He knocked once, and I pulled open the door.

I took my time lifting my gaze off his broad chest to meet his eyes. Already he wore the look I saved to memory. The one that left nothing up for question. He wanted me.

Jayce leaned on the panel of my door, his eyes coasting over my curves. His arm abandoned his side, which he used to loop around me to pull me close. I obliged, closing my eyes when his warm breath brushed against my lips.

"I've been waiting and wanting to do this to you all day." He pressed his lips against mine and I lost all strength to resist. Why would I? Earth stopped spinning whenever he kissed me. The first time I experienced this truth, I thought it was because it was our first kiss. But every time he crushed his lips against mine, the act got better and I found myself even more grounded in his power of now.

He backed me into the apartment and when we were inside, he closed the door with his foot. With my back to the door, Jayce ravished me. His tongue lapped against mine, massaging the length of it then drawing it into his mouth and sucking on it. I may have been able to hold back with him for eight semesters, avoiding eye contact, limiting our conversations. These days, though, it was impossible.

I moaned on his lips like he was inside me. The way his tongue moved against mine and the grip of his hands on my ass sure felt that way.

He walked me away from the door and over to the side table beside the floor-length mirror. With just one swipe, he knocked my keys and a stack of mail to the ground to make room for me. Jayce placed me on the table and immediately pushed the hem of my skirt up my hips, his fingers gripping the side seams of my panties with the hook of his fingers. The entire time he kept his lips on mine, his tongue-glides never faltered as he managed to multi-task like a boss.

With my panties off and his pants down at his ankles, Jayce leaned back to tear open the condom wrapper, his focus locked on mine. His lids were heavy, the sex in his eyes heightened by lust. He probably wouldn't believe me if I told him I'd never experienced *this* before. *This* kind of passion, *this* brand of need.

Sheathed, he grabbed my thighs and pulled me close. Pressed his palm to the wall above my head and guided himself between my walls.

"God, you're wet," he whispered. "I got you wet like this?"

I couldn't respond, didn't care to. The way he made me stretch around the column of his dick always sent me over the edge. I folded my lips in my mouth as I rocked with him to his rhythm, desperately in search of the crescendo I never thought were possible to reach without my clit receiving equal attention.

He held my right hip tight when he found his pace. Locked eyes with me as my walls remembered him, molding to his width. I bit my bottom lip and tossed my head back, letting go and allowing him to take total control. During the day, I competed with Jayce at *BBA*. Constantly thought of ways to one-up him because out of all the other interns he was indeed the smartest. I wasn't sure how that was possible. He was a jock, a frat boy. But he *was* the brightest of the interns. And though I didn't want to admit it, he intrigued me. Pair that with the fact he had my walls fluttering around his staff once more, my breath hitched in my throat as he buried himself in me to the hilt, making me come undone yet again. I was slowly becoming addicted.

He grabbed my jaw and used it to lower my head so our eyes met.

"I love when I get you like this," he confessed through his moans. "Hot, wet, whining, and panting for something only I can give you in this moment."

I cried out and didn't recognize my voice. Vulnerability and desperation raised my pitch two octaves.

With his hands still on my jaw, he kissed me while still fucking me. Doing that thing that drove me wild, stroking my tongue the same way his dick stroked my pussy.

I whimpered against his lips and clutched the edge of my table with my fingers.

Just as fast, Jayce picked me up and walked me to the opposite wall, and held me up against it. He pinned me to the surface and quickened his pace, his upstrokes direct and accurate. He wined against me, moving his hips counterclockwise to my enjoyment. The man refused to let up off my sweet spot for even a second.

Jayce held me against the wall with one arm that he snaked up my back to hold me in place. His fingers gripped my shoulder, which he used to pull me down as he thrusted upward so I would meet his upstrokes.

My eyes rolled, legs trembled, and everything became blurry.

"Fuck, Summer," he whispered against my neck. "Come baby."

And I did, loudly, while shaking uncontrollably. It's a wonder how he could keep me in place, but he did until he got his too.

In the middle of trying to catch my breath, he leaned his forehead against mine and inhaled my ragged exhales. He pecked my lips next as he stepped out of his pants, then wrapped my legs around his waist.

"You want more?" he asked as he walked me to my bed. "Because I got a lot more to give."

All I did was nod, knowing it wasn't at all a bluff. Jayce intended to make this a long night, and that unspoken plan had me grinning on his lips.

TEN

JAYCE

The sun had risen an hour prior when I twisted my head to lay eyes on her. She'd fallen asleep minutes after our third round hours ago. Now she laid beside me in bed, spent. I don't know what it was about Summer that got me like that. My strong attraction to her could be because of her slick mouth or stuck up attitude. Ironically, those were the two things I thought I liked least about her. I don't know, call me crazy, but in my mind I believed I had the ability to fuck some change into her.

I chuckled at the thought. My eyes wandered around her room. Summer's apartment was that of a pampered princess. Large Victorian upholstered bed, two mirrors on either side of her mattress with vanity light bulbs framing the edges of them. Powder pink and white bedding. From the looks of it, she had an obsession with vintage Hollywood or something.

Anyway, sex with Summer, I realized, was the only opportunity I had to humble her. Knowing I could get her to chill out and be something other than what she showed me off the bed – hell, what she showed others, period - made my involvement with her exciting.

Was this an involvement?

I honestly thought it would have been one night. Smash and move on like I did the rest. Not with her though. Even as I laid in her room beside her, knowing I'd need to get up and head back to my apartment in Harlem, I wanted to slide between her walls again.

I showed up at her place the previous night. Didn't even head home first, just came straight here. The thirst was real.

I ran my hand from my forehead, down over my nose, and finished at my lips where I held them in a gentle pinch.

The way she wrapped around me last night and the night a few weeks ago was all the indication I needed to know she ain't never had a man like me. That was perfect. Because I ain't never had a woman like her either... ever.

She rolled off her side and laid flat on her back. Her head turned in my direction next. Finally, her lids peeled opened. Black hair laid sprawled across her face, covering most of it. I saw her eyes blink a little through the blur of her hair. A smile pulled at her lips next. Her million-dollar grin was so spine-tingling. It's a shame she didn't share it much.

"Stalker," she whispered.

I laughed.

Summer brushed her hair out of her face to reveal a morning glow like no other. Shorty was so bad. Her powder pink flat sheet laid contoured against her naked frame like silk.

"Is that what you do?" She turned on her side to face me again. "Stare at people when they sleep?"

"You were snoring." I lied. "Really loud, too."

She gasped. "Shut up! I was not."

I snorted a laugh.

The two of us laid in bed for a moment longer. I thought back to the day before in the break room when that guy interrupted us.

I sucked the tip of my tongue against my top teeth, not wanting to ask but doing it, anyway.

"So... he asked you out?"

Her eyes rolled up to meet mine. In them I knew she knew exactly *what* and *who* I was talking about.

"So... are you jealous?" A big smile crested her lips and my heart damn near beat out of my chest.

She's gonna mess around and make me fuck her again just to teach her a lesson.

I pointed at my bare chest. "Me? Jealous?" I shrugged the corners of my lips. "Nah."

"Oh... kay."

"I got plenty of other *friends*," I said with finger quotes, "who I could have called last night but I wanted to spend that time with you."

A frown threatened to pull her lips down, but she fought the weight of her disappointment well and flashed a convincing smile instead.

"Good because..." She pressed her hand into her mattress to lean her back against her white tufted headboard, the sheet falling off one breast. "That means you understand there's no potential for there to be anything more between us besides this, right?"

"Of course," I replied. I sincerely never thought past the sex with Summer. Getting between her legs had been a central focus for two semesters until I realized she would require too much work and I wasn't going to focus hard on anything that interfered with school or getting this money to buy my family a house. But now, with school out of the way, the cash almost secured for a down payment, and my internship running smoothly, I kind of had a change of heart.

"But..." I started, sitting up to press my back to her headboard too. "Why do you say that?"

She furrowed her brows. As if me asking that was the most absurd thing she heard all week.

She said, "Our backgrounds are in stark contrast."

My eyes roamed off hers and into her living room, falling on fashion and beauty magazines stacked one on top of the other on her coffee table surrounded by artisan candles. All of that sat under a large sparkling chandelier.

On her walls were crystal framed photos of herself and a woman who resembled her but appeared slightly more tan than Summer's fair complexion. The fanciest thing in my apartment was a ceiling fan, and that joint didn't even work. Yeah, we were different, *way* different, and that obvious fact was unmistakable.

But... so what?

"And your background with that guy at the office is more of a match?"

"He's a junior partner." She beamed. "He has his own office, with a cute enough view. He graduated from an Ivy League and his family vacations at Martha's Vineyard. Oh! And his folks own two wineries, a bakery and four—"

"Aight, aight." I waved her off. "I get it."

I clenched my jaw and loosened the tension the second I realized I was getting upset.

Why the hell was I getting upset?

"Anyway." I rolled off the bed and on to my feet. "I have to head back to my apartment to shower and get my head right for work."

She grabbed the flat sheet and pulled the bedding higher over her naked breasts. "Do you live nearby?"

I stepped into my boxers, then my trousers from the day before and made my way to her side of the bed. With my palms pressed into the cushion of the mattress, I leaned in close, bringing my lips to her neck. "You're smart enough to know we come from different backgrounds so I know you know I don't *live* nearby." I kissed her there, and she shivered immediately.

I moved out of her space while buckling my pants, smiling to myself, pleased with her reaction.

"My place is in Harlem," I informed. "So, it isn't *nearby*, but my apartment isn't too far from here either."

"Okay. Um..." She ran her palm along the back of her neck. "Thanks for last night."

I stopped in my stride toward her front door to grab my shirt and leave. When I turned to face her, I took note of the slight smile on her lips.

"Did Ms. Summer McKoy just show gratitude for something?"

She kissed her teeth. "Okay, get out."

I pointed at her and winked. "Now, that sounds more like the woman I know."

———

Hours later and at *BBA's* conference table, I rolled my head around my neck twice in search of relief. The new case with Melissa Hatchett had become a monumental one for the firm... exhausting, too. Outside of the offices, me and the other interns had to damn near swim through the sea of press camped out in front of the building.

After it was confirmed that *Brown, Bloom & Associates* took on her case, news outlets sent their hungriest journalists to gather as much detail about what the firm was planning to go head-to-head with the prosecution team.

It had only been close to two weeks since we got our first assignment to draft up questions to ask during Jeff's cross examination in court in a few days. Now, we had to decide on our next move.

"We could continue digging up dirt about the officer," David, one intern suggested.

Jeff walked into the conference room a few minutes earlier, asking us to read his mind. Tell him what we think we should do next for the case. It was his way of fielding ideas on how to set this case in motion, so the evidence worked in Melissa's favor.

"Impossible," Jeff spat. "Officer Esposito was a modeled citizen in front of eyes. There's no way that would fly."

"Let's have Melissa speak to the press," Summer suggested. "Give her side of the story. The world loves a sob story and needs to form a connection to her. She's still grieving since she lost her fiancé hours before they were to exchange vows. She'll get a chance to shape the public's perception and will silence the idea that she's some kind of monster."

"That's an excellent suggestion, Summer, but Melissa wants nothing to do with the press," Jeff stated. "She's vilified them and blamed journalists and reporters for creating a narrative for the case that she believes will influence the jury negatively. The only place she's willing to talk is inside a closed courtroom."

"Then we should organize a focus group," I spoke next. "Offer a mock trial comprising only of her peers."

"Hmm," Jeff hummed. "That sounds better than what I was thinking. Go on."

"At the end of the mock trial, have those participants give their feedbacks on Melissa's responses. Strangers pick up on subtle nuances that influence a person's level of likability. The participants can help with identifying them without bias. This will also be a great way to prep her for trial, so she's familiar with what to expect. And give us an opportunity to filter out any detrimental verbiage or reactions, allowing us to school her on how to translate and respond to the prosecution's questions in court."

Jeff snapped his fingers and pointed at me. "Yes! That's the one. Give me an hour or two to put out a call to gather a few participants. I'll come up with specific questions I want you all to ask during the session and I'll have Stephanie divvy those questions up amongst the group."

Jeff clapped his hands once. "Good job, Jayce. Very good job."

My heart swelled with so much pride but I swallowed it back only offering a modest head nod.

Jeff left the room when I said, "Y'all don't hurt yourselves being more like me, okay?"

The room erupted in giggles. Summer rolled her eyes while trying to fight back her smile.

I stretched my arms high above my head, a yawn expanding the back of my throat as I let my exhaustion out audibly.

"Long night?" Veronika asked beside me.

I had to give it to her. She was persistent. For the past few days, she'd been laying her attraction to me on thick. No longer was she dropping hints. She was slowly moving in for the kill.

My eyes shifted over to Summer who stared at us from her seat at the other head of the table. Noticing my gaze on hers, Summer cocked a brow.

"Yeah," I confirmed, my view still on Summer. "A really *long* night."

Summer smiled big across from me, tiny dimples dotting the sides of her cheeks.

Veronika followed my line of vision to Summer, and I noticed when Veronika's face contorted for only a moment.

"Let's grab drinks after this at *GrayArea,*" she suggested, placing her hand on mine.

I focused down on her grip.

"We can discuss the case, throw around a few ideas between us that we think Jeff will find useful."

My first thought was to decline her offer. With all honesty, it was a Friday. I hadn't planned on it, but I definitely wouldn't have been against the idea of heading back to Summer's apartment to count how many more times I could make her scream *God* in my ear. But she made it crystal clear earlier that morning there could be nothing more between us besides bed sheets. So, why show loyalty to her?

"Yeah, let's do that," I said to Veronika, then shifted my eyes back to Summer.

Summer squinted her eyes my way, and I shrugged my brows. She responded by rolling her eyes hard at me, balling her lips, then focusing down on the stack of papers in front of her, suddenly interested in getting back to work.

Shorty really had some nerve. She had no problem accepting dates from junior partner Anton. Summer pretty much told me I wasn't good enough for her, but she wanted to get in her feelings when I accept an invitation for drinks from a woman who a blind man could tell was a knockout just like her.

She had me fucked up.

———

Night had set the scene for the p.m. hours in New York City. The after-work crowd poured into *GrayArea's* lounge and bar by the droves. The establishment impressed Veronika when we visited as a group for the welcome dinner so she insisted we return specifically to the bar for drinks.

"What's going on with you and Summer?" she asked.

We weren't even at the bar for a whole five minutes before she jumped right to the point.

I smirked. "I thought discussing the case was the plan tonight."

She smiled, her umber-brown skin glowing beneath the bar's ceiling lights. "I'm just curious." She shrugged. "I always catch you two exchanging glances but never really talk to each other at the office. She's a real bitch, so I'm surprised she's caught your eye."

I lifted my cognac to my lips to sample. "Harsh words."

"That girl is impossible." Veronika brought the rim of her wine glass to her lips to sip her Chardonnay. "She acts like the world revolves around her. As if she's too good to be in the company of others. Which is why I'm so surprised she's set her sights on you."

I jerked my head back. "What do you mean by that?"

"Summer is always staring at you with little hearts in her eyes like some sort of living emoji. I swear you're like her main focus."

If I could blush, I would have. Instead I said, "And how do you know where she's staring?"

"Because I'm looking that way too." She winked.

"I see."

"It's just that... she's so *uppity*," Veronika continued. "Very Fifth Avenue and Madison, high-yellow-passe-blanc, prissy city girl. She won't shut up about her father, Mr. King of New York and how he owns this, that, and the third."

I nodded. "True."

"Then there's... you." Veronika ran her fingertips up the fabric of my shirt that covered my bicep. I'd loosened my tie and rolled up my sleeves to my forearms the moment we walked through *GrayArea's* double glass doors. "You're so laid back, unbelievably handsome of course, smart but not obnoxious about it which you should be, we *are* competing for only *one* job."

I shrugged the corners of my lips.

"What on earth do you see in Summer McKoy?"

"A lot," Summer's voice chirped from behind us.

Veronika and I both turned in our seats on our respective bar stools to see Summer standing there. Dressed in her gray pencil skirt and matching blazer with a powder pink sleeveless blouse beneath, cleavage in full view. Her hips swayed as she placed one foot in front of the other, closing the space between us. "I love when I'm the topic of conversation just in time for me to join in."

"Join in?!" Veronika spat. "What the hell are you even doing here?"

"I figured I'd come and grab drinks with you guys," she explained, her eyes on mine.

"Ha! That's funny. Not a soul invited you though," Veronika snarled through her teeth.

"Nonsense," Summer purred. She licked her lips slowly and blood rushed to my dick instantly. "I'm like *Visa*, accepted any and everywhere I go."

I pushed the tip of my tongue toward my back molar and let the smile on my lips appear. Summer was so audacious. That shit was beyond sexy to me.

Veronika exhaled sharply to my right as Summer grabbed a seat on the bar stool to my left.

Summer placed her designer leather bag on the counter. "I see you two have already ordered."

"*Yes*," Veronika hissed. "Because I planned for it to be only *us* two."

"And now it's *us* three. Be a big girl and adjust, 'kay?" Summer raised a hand to the bartender. "Hi, I'll take a whiskey sour on ice."

"You and your hard drinks," I said to her.

She honed those feline brown eyes on mine. They were smoldering and dark with want.

"Well," she whispered. "You out of all people should know how much I *love* hard things."

I groaned, folding my bottom lip into my mouth and biting down on it to keep myself from pouncing on her.

"Ladies drink wine," Veronika taunted to my right. I glanced that way, then dropped my eyes to the bar's counter, picking up my glass of cognac and taking a bigger sip than normal. It was clear where this exchange was going.

"Oh, yeah?" Summer replied as she accepted her drink from the bartender. "Then why exactly are *you* drinking wine?"

"Queens, please," I tried.

Veronika kissed her teeth. She picked up her glass of wine next and finished what was left. "I'm out of here." On her feet, she leaned in close and whispered in my ear, "Call me when you're done playing with her." She leaned away and made eye contact with Summer before rolling her eyes and walking off.

"What are you doing here?" I asked Summer once we were alone.

"Saving you." She sipped her whiskey. I found it intriguing how she never cringed while drinking something so spirited. "You couldn't possibly be enjoying your time with her, no matter how short it must have been."

I shrugged, taking another sip of my drink. "She's more my speed. We have similar backgrounds."

Summer whipped her head in my direction and glared at me with narrowed eyes. I returned her glare until she turned her head away, picked up her glass and tossed the mixed drink back, finishing everything in one gulp.

"Bartender." She held up a finger. "Another, please. This time only whiskey, no sour."

"Be easy, ma," I warned. "I'm not trying to carry you out of here."

"This," she replied, accepting her second drink, "is light work. They water the whiskey down here. Show concern if I'm pouring from my own personal bottle."

She tossed back the second glass, and my hard-on strained against my trouser's fly after baring witness to her gall.

Anton the junior partner could have his weak ass date with her. But tonight, the four walls in her apartment would hear my name and mine alone.

ELEVEN

"Let's share a cab," Jayce suggested the moment we stepped out of the bar. After my third drink, I agreed that I'd had enough, and it was time to go. Veronika really thought I would let her show me up tonight. She understood what she was doing, inviting him out for drinks to discuss *the case*. Yeah, sure. From our very first day at *Brown, Bloom & Associates,* she's had eyes for Jayce. Ogling him, always wanting to sit beside him.

Ugh.

Whatever.

I shouldn't care, right?

Right...

... right?

I mean, deep down, I was well aware this thing with Jayce couldn't go any further than where it was now. So why *did* I care who he had drinks with? So much so, I would show up at the bar, uninvited, as pointed out by *her*, to crash their little... whatever it was.

Jayce and I fell into our seats when I successfully flagged a yellow cab down a block from *GrayArea.*

"So, are you going to tell me what that really was in there?" he asked.

"I told you." I squeezed my bag between my left hip and the door. "I was saving you."

"Really, Summer?"

"Yes, really." I kissed my teeth. "She's not even your type."

"And what's my type."

"Me. You said so yourself during the welcome dinner."

He scoffed.

"Am I supposed to ignore the fact the girl you described was me? Besides." I shrugged. "I'm every man's type."

The night was your typical humid hot summer night, but I was even hotter inside, pissed that Jayce was giving a girl like Veronika hope. Why was he even leading Veronika on?

Was he leading her on?

"Are you leading her on?" I asked out loud.

"Leading her—" He paused his speech to run his hand down his jaw. "You tell me we can't have more than what we have now because of our backgrounds, then you crash a drink date with a colleague after convincing yourself I needed *saving*, or as you claimed, because she isn't my type. Veronika is actually really cool. I dig her company... type or not."

I scoffed. "*Drink date*? *Dig her company*? Who are you kidding?"

He laughed while looking away. "I can't quite grasp your motive, shorty, *at all*." Jayce glanced my way again and added, "You're confusing me in the worse way because your mouth is telling me one thing but your actions are contradicting as hell."

I buried my lips in my mouth while shaking my head.

"You want me but don't really want me and when someone else is putting it out there that they want me, here you go cock blocking."

I pointed at myself. "Who? Me? A cock blocker?"

"Hell yeah."

"You planned to fuck her tonight, didn't you?!" I shrieked. The cab driver peeked at us through his rear-view mirror, and Jayce held a hand up apologetically.

"First, lower your voice in mixed company." He gestured at the cabbie. "Second, I didn't say all that. But if one thing led to another and if Roni and I were tuned in to that frequency, I don't see why not."

"Roni," I mumbled as I rolled my eyes away from his. "Typical. I heard you used to bang a few of your professors and their teacher aides, so you toying with the idea of juggling two women doesn't surprise me in the least."

"You know what you just said has nothing to do with this, right? It's actually random as fuck. You know that, right?"

I angled my chin up to keep face.

"And you seem to enjoy the benefits of all that I've learned from my *professors* and *teacher aides*, so *why* are you trippin' sweetheart?"

My jaw dropped as I whipped my head to my right to shoot a bullet glare his way. "No you did not just say that."

He chuckled, running his hand down the frame of his lips. "Look, Summer, I'm feeling you, I want you to know that, aight? But this is *not* a relationship. Far from it. We're doing us. And when we're *not* together, best believe *I will* be doing me. Whether that be with Veronika or any other beautiful woman. Just like you'll be doing the same with Anton, the junior partner."

"Oh, come on," I whispered. "Is this what this is about? Why you're even glancing Veronika's way?"

He shrugged. "I didn't make the rules. You had me under the impression there was an understanding between us. Do we not still have the same understanding?"

"We do." I blinked my eyes away.

We did.

It's just that Jayce *did* something to me other guys in my past never succeeded at. Was I wrong for wanting him all to myself and possibly going to war over what we have, even if *I* made it clear we could never have more than *that*?

And don't say yes.

I had boyfriends, not so much after enrolling at *Langston University*. Graduating with top honors was my focus. It was an easy focus since my mother made it clear not to bother myself with any of the guys on campus because of where most of them came from.

Everything I'd ever done, I made it a priority to be the best at it, anyway. Reading, which I started doing at 2-years-old. Ballet, which I studied from the age of six to eighteen, I excelled at. So much so, I performed in a solo act a week before my high school graduation to a roaring applause.

In my high school studies, I was always the best in my class. I would've been valedictorian if I didn't have a high school sweetheart. With my head up in the clouds, he bested me by obtaining a one point higher GPA, making me salutatorian. That's why when I started my first year at *LU,* I denounced boys. Told myself if I involved myself with them, it would only be on a physical level so I wouldn't get distracted from my studies. Seeing Jayce on campus almost delayed that, but I remained disciplined and it's a good thing I did because I was falling for him now, and hard.

For most of the ride, the two of us remained silent. I didn't know what to say to him, and apparently neither did he. I wondered what thoughts ran through his mind.

"What's got you so quiet?" I asked him.

"How did you determine that we don't come from the same background?"

The question took me aback. In that moment, I realized my words may have really bothered him. More than I expected.

I was never one to mince words though.

"Well," I began, "first, the way you talk. You're able to turn it off a bit at *BBA,* but it's easy to tell you're from the inner city."

"And what's wrong with being from the *inner city*?"

"Nothing, really, except it's just not where I pictured the guy of my dreams growing up."

He turned his face to me. Jayce was the most handsome man I'd ever laid eyes on, and I could say that honestly and wholeheartedly. Strong jawline, piercing dark eyes, lips so plump and juicy it took all of me not to press mine against his whenever I was around him these days. He had the body of a god - squared shoulders, hulking biceps, and height that was sexy all on its own. The one thing that has always melted my heart, his smile, was missing though.

"The guy of your dreams, huh?" he questioned.

I bit my tongue to keep from elaborating.

"Are you saying you're too good for me, Summer?"

I shifted my eyes away from his and bit my lips closed.

"Because that's what it sounds like you're alluding to... that you think you're too good for me to have as mine and mine alone."

I focused my eyes out the window to my left. "We're just different, Jayce."

"That doesn't answer my question."

I closed my eyes and turned my head to face him again. My eyes opened to his when I said, "No, I don't *think* I'm too good for you, Jayce. I *know* I am."

"Damn!" He blew out a long flow of air while leaning back in his seat. Soon a laugh bellowed from his gut, and he covered his mouth with his fist. "You know... for a woman with a name that hints at warmth, you sure are ice cold, baby."

The cab driver turned onto my block, and the brownstone that housed my studio apartment came into view.

"West 89th Street," the driver announced from behind the wheel.

"Thank you." I lifted my purse to my lap to dip my hand inside to retrieve my wallet. "You can pull over right here in front of 278."

Jayce grabbed my wrist, stopping me.

"I got it," he said.

"Are you coming up?" I asked, my eyes boring into his.

"Nah, you go 'head." He focused forward. "I'll see you on Monday."

I pursed my lips and grabbed the handle of the door to open it and exit the car.

Before my foot could touch the first step leading up to the front door of the brownstone, the taxi drove away with Jayce still in the backseat.

TWELVE

The cab rolled up the road and away from Summer's brownstone when I chuckled to myself.

"Yo, my man," I called to the driver, slipping a twenty out of my leather slimfold wallet. "You can let me down here."

I wasn't good enough for her.

This wasn't new news to me. I knew Summer thought this way. Why else would she act how she's been acting all these years?

I paid the cabbie and stepped out of the car, then headed in the opposite direction, back to Summer's apartment.

She needed to cool off. I loved her confidence, adored her feisty nature, but she wasn't dealing with any ordinary man.

I wouldn't allow myself to be that predictable. She was fine, that was true, and I wanted her a lot more these days. But I also knew my worth, just like she knew hers. I just didn't need to treat people like shit to show it. Something deeper was pulling us together, but she was going to put some respect on our dealings if I had anything to do with her. That was nonnegotiable.

In front of her building, I tilted my head back to glance up at the window on the top floor. The lights were still on, so I knew she hadn't turned in yet.

I pulled my phone out of my pocket and tapped on her name in my call log while taking steps up the staircase. She answered after the first ring.

"Yes?"

"Had enough time to think?" I asked as I leaned on the front door. The neighborhood was made for cinematic backdrops. Well-structured brownstones with classy flowers planted for the season. For a New York City block, it was quieter than the average.

"To think about what?"

I chuckled. "Buzz me in. I'm downstairs."

I heard the subtle gasp on the other end of the phone. Picking up on that made me smile. Soon, the hum of the door's buzzer sounded, and I pulled the door open and made my way upstairs.

As I climbed the final case of stairs to her apartment, her legs came into view the higher I rose. Summer's stems were thick and shapely. Her body was something to do a double take at, but I had this thing for legs and ass and Summer had a lot of both.

She rubbed her lips together when our eyes met. I approached her.

"I see you changed your mind," she purred. There was something different in her eyes in that moment. Innocence and an undeniable presence of want she had no intention of hiding. This was the most vulnerable I think I'd ever seen her. Actually, I *know* she's never been this vulnerable in front of me or anyone else. The more time we spent together, the more her walls seemed to crumble around me.

Close, I cradled her jaw in my hand and leaned her head back to press my lips to hers. Her eyes collapsed closed. Summer moved closer to me, pressing her breasts to my ribs and wrapping her arms around my waist. She felt good here, in my space and me in hers.

I bent my legs at the knees, gripped her thighs and picked her up.

Inside her apartment, I shut the door and turned to hold her up against the wall beside it as I twisted the locks.

"Why'd you leave?" she whispered on my lips.

"I had a point to prove," I retorted.

She tightened her legs around my waist as I walked her over to her bed, my usual stroll in her apartment. The weight of her in my arms satisfied something in me I couldn't name. I'd never experienced this kind of affection. A kiss, yes. Sex, definitely. But this sensation, the one that made me want to give this woman the world just to make her smile? I've never been here before. I liked it a lot.

What is this? I wondered to myself as I laid her on her back and pressed my body to hers. Our tongues wrestled in our mouths. Her hands clasped the sides of my face as she moaned on my lips, eyes closed, just so into me the way I was into her.

I gently broke our kiss to trail kisses down to her neck.

"Jayce?" she voiced.

"Yeah, Summer?"

"No one has ever made me do the things you make me do, what you make me...*feel*."

I peeked up at her to see her biting at her lips in thought. "Elaborate."

She rolled her eyes.

I lifted away and planted my forearms on either side of her, caging her in and hovering over her frame.

"Please don't make me have to explain what I meant."

I grinned, and she snorted a laugh.

"Out with it," I pushed.

"Physically," she started.

"Physically, what?"

Summer sighed then blurted, "I never *came* with anybody else."

I cocked a brow.

"Clitoral, yes, I can get myself off. But not the other way and not in the way *you* make me do it." Her eyes darted from left to right in search of a reaction.

I knew it. She shocked me admitting it, but I knew all along. The way she moaned with angst, how she clung to me when she reached that peak, the hold her walls had around my dick, they were all telling signs she'd never.

I stared at her for a moment and she looked away shyly. "Don't let that go to your head though. I just thought I'd let you know. Give you insight as to why I would be so... territorial. Tell anyone and it'll be the last thing you tell."

A smirk pulled at my lips that made her laugh, flashing that smile that did things to me I couldn't understand.

"How? How have *you* never—" I questioned. "All this mouth you got with everything else, I would think—"

"I lost my virginity right before I started college. My mother explained that an orgasm would probably happen later on since this was all new to me."

I furrowed my brows. "You told your mother?!"

She shrugged. "She's my best friend. I tell her everything." Summer rolled her eyes closed. "*Almost* everything."

"So, you've never had an organism from intercourse before." I licked my lips while moving a hand down between us, pressing my fingers against the crotch of her black varsity shorts.

She gasped.

"You should have never told me that." I smiled. "Because now, I'm gonna have a lot more fun with you."

Her cat eyes widened.

"Let's see if you can handle being schooled by me."

I clasped my hands to the shape of her pussy as my fingers massaged the space where her slit hid behind fabric.

She inhaled sharply in response.

"First important lesson," I began as I leaned back on my haunches and pulled at her varsity shorts and then her panties, removing them both. "In sex, you are either the teacher or the student."

She laid there wearing only her white tank top, naked below the waist, her thin landing strip in full view. I swiped my tongue along my bottom lip at the beautiful sight.

"Sometimes," I continued, planting one arm beside her arm while hovering over her and gliding my hand down to her sex, "the roles alternate, often while in the act. You teach by showing me what you like, and I learn by studying what actions make you call me God. For it to be good between us, someone always has to be teaching while the other is eagerly learning."

Summer closed her eyes and arched her back.

I lowered myself down beside her. Kept her legs spread opened for me by placing my knee between them. Laying at her side, I glided two fingers inside her and she gasped as they entered.

"Next lesson, this one exclusive to me though."

She moaned.

"I can make you come with just about any part of me, Summer. You know that right?"

Her breaths became heavy the more I worked my fingers in her and curved them at the tips in a *come to me* gesture to invite her orgasm to flow.

"With this..." I swiped my tongue along the shell of her ear. "With my dick – a fact you're very familiar with."

She inhaled a shaky breath.

"And with these two digits right here and doing only this."

Her walls pulsed like heartbeats around my fingers, so I moved them in another inch and toyed with the sponge of her G-spot.

"God," she whispered.

"Mm-hmm, there it is." I whispered back. "You feel that, huh?"

She nodded, still moaning.

With my free hand, I hiked up her tank, took her nipple in my mouth, and sucked on the light brown morsel while still pleasing her with the length of my fingers.

Her back arched even more off her bed as she fed her nipple to me, gyrating her wet pussy against my hand.

"I think I'm coming," she announced low before sucking her bottom lip into her mouth and squeezing her eyes shut.

"Yeah," I breathed, watching in awe as her body shuddered. "You definitely are."

I curved my finger a centimeter more and massaged her G-spot until she was so caught up in coming, no sound escaped her lips. She kept inhaling and forgetting to exhale. Her body shook though. The walls inside her fluttered so much it was like she was trying to suck me in.

And when it hit, her orgasm, she released the longest, loudest, breathiest moan I'd ever heard her make and my dick grew so hard it hurt to keep it in my pants.

Her body quaked uncontrollably, even after I removed my fingers and lowered my face to her pussy.

The swipe of my tongue against her clit had her trying to crawl away, but I held her still by the legs.

"Final lesson: never run. If you do, you'll cheat yourself out of coming," I told her right before diving back in.

I licked and sucked, tongue kissing her tiny pink button as she mindlessly strained her vocal chords. Her thighs squeezed either side of my face as her hands held my head in place. I loved her scent, the way she tasted. Didn't think there was anything about this woman that didn't infatuate me. I especially loved it when she succumbed to ecstasy produced by my actions.

My tongue licked her to another screaming orgasm when her arms collapsed at her sides and she laid there spent.

I pulled off my pants, unwrapped a condom, and turned her over by the legs. Licked her from the back of her thighs, over the mound of her ass, up her back and stopped at her ear to ask, "Are you still here with me, Ms. McKoy?"

All she could do was let out a moan.

I chuckled while running my sheathed head against her wet opening from the back. She was so slick, making it easy for me to glide right in. Summer reached for her pillow covered in a powder pink pillow case and buried her face in the cushion completely, exhaling a lengthy growl.

I pumped my hips back and forth then created figure eights slowly on top of her. She poked her ass up to meet each stroke. Our moans were in sync now as I worked to get us both to that place of no return.

Someone else staking claim to *this*, experiencing her in *this* way, ran laps through my mind. It was like those menacing thoughts wore metal cleats, leaving impressions in my conscience of her intimate moments with them that didn't yet occur. But the thoughts sure had a real effect in my mind, making me clench my jaw as if she were sleeping with anyone besides me. Her holding anyone else that wasn't me snug between her thighs made me grind my teeth and bury myself deeper inside of her.

I grabbed her wrists and gathered them above her head as I sped up. The sound of our bodies meeting clapped around the apartment, the noise in competition with our moans.

"You don't understand what you do to me," I told her.

I licked my lips and savored her there.

Those walls of hers began fluttering again, and her body grew stiff beneath me.

A rush pulled at my gut, and I hardened inside of her. My dick jumped, and I squeezed my grip around her wrist tighter, continuing my movements in and out of her as we spiraled through our release together.

I pressed my face to the back of her head and roared my moan into her hair while I pumped my hips back and forth, only stopping when I had no energy left to give. I gained control over my breath though by breathing her in and out. She held my face in place, clasping her palm to the nape of my neck.

"Damn, Summer," I whispered through exhales. "What are you doing to me, baby?"

Thirteen

"Tell me something I don't know about you," Jayce propositioned beside me.

I turned my head to look at him, then rolled my eyes away shyly. "If you don't know it, then you weren't supposed to."

It was the next day, a Saturday, and the day after summer officially started. My namesake. I was born in the summer, in August. This was my mother's favorite season, so she named her firstborn after it.

"Come on," he bumped his shoulder with mine. "Tell me."

Jayce and I had just had sex for the millionth time that morning. Well, perhaps not the millionth, but I'd honestly lost count of the amount of times we went at it. The man just couldn't get enough. How he conjured up the energy and the blood flow to maintain a hard-on after several rounds prior was beyond my understanding at that point. The man was insatiable, and I wasn't complaining one bit.

I focused up at the ceiling and exhaled sharply through my nose. "I used to practice ballet."

His brows rose. "You?"

I nodded. "From the time I was six and until my final year in high school. Even performed in a solo show two weeks before my high school graduation. It was a big deal."

That day was the happiest and saddest day of my life. I'd practiced feverishly, competed like a beast to land the solo part. My mother promised me that my father would be in attendance. I hadn't seen him in years and worked even harder to impress him for weeks leading up to the event only for him to be a no-show. But everyone raved about my performance and from what I hear the performance became the proto-type for what the studio expected from students. Dance instructors pressed play on my performance video for newcomers when they arrived for their first lesson.

"Why'd you stop?" he asked.

Because my father stood me up, is what I wanted to say. Instead I opted for, "Just lost interest, I guess. I still practice from time to time at *Obsidian Sports Center* in Brooklyn. My mother is friends with the owner's mother. They have a nice dance studio. I go there whenever I need to clear my head."

"Hmph." Jayce pulled at the flat sheet covering my legs and stared down at my feet. "Your toes aren't that of a ballerina's. Those women work really hard and it often shows."

"Weekly trips to a famed podiatrist to the stars prevents that." I wiggled my toes. "My mother wouldn't have it any other way."

He snorted a laugh.

"Your turn," I said to him. "Tell me something."

He turned to face me. After rubbing his lips together a few times in contemplation he said, "I got about $42,000 saved up for a down payment on a house for my mother and siblings."

My jaw dropped.

"I found this program for first-time home buyers that will cover the rest. I just need about eight grand more for the down deposit." He smiled big. "I'm close."

"Hmm," I hummed once I was struck with a thought. "*Brown, Bloom & Associates* kind of *close*?"

A sly grin tugged at one corner of his mouth. "I plead the fifth."

I shoved him playfully. "How did you get $42,000, anyway? Did you have a job while attending *LU*?"

"Nah, not quite." He sat up to press his back to my headboard. "I used to write class papers for most of the guys on the team and they'd pay me. Doing that, saving what was left from my scholarship money every semester, and selling digital art online helped me rack up the rest. I just kept saving without looking at the total, and when I finally did, I realized it amounted to that."

"Wait, write *their* papers?" I challenged. "I always thought you were paying people to write yours."

"Nope." He shook his head. "I used to write theirs and mine."

"And you're an artist, too?!"

He grinned. "Nah, not really. I'm just a whiz with illustrating software is all."

"Jayce!" I leaned my back against the headboard too. "That's amazing."

"It's aight," he said matter-of-factly, then smirked.

I laughed.

My eyes rolled up his arm. Visible veins mapped his virility, lining his forearm. I stopped my visual tour at his bicep. There laid a flat scar in the shape of a Greek letter.

I outlined the letter with my fingertip. "Tell me about this."

He flexed his bicep, and I licked my lips at the pronounced bulge in his arm that suddenly appeared.

"I got it right after I joined my frat."

"Why?"

He peered down at me.

"Why brand yourself like this?" I quizzed.

"The decision is a form of self-sacrifice and the love I have for my frat. Till I die." He twisted his wrist, framed his face, and barked like the brothers from his fraternity often did. His barks traveling around my apartment.

"Oh, God." I rolled my eyes. "Please don't start stepping in here. This is imported hardwood."

He laughed from his gut.

Tap, tap, tap!

Both of our heads turned to my front door. I wrinkled my brows as I turned to my right to check the time on my digital alarm clock.

9:30 a.m.

"Expecting somebody?" he asked.

"I don't think so," I said back. I asked toward the door, "Who is it?"

"Summer, doll, it's me! Open up."

I gasped, cupping my hand over my mouth. "Oh, shit!"

"What?"

I was on my feet, grabbing his clothes off my floor and tossing them one by one in his direction. "It's my *mother*. You have to get up and get out!"

Jayce was on his feet, too, pulling on his garments quicker than I could finish my sentence. All he heard was "mother" before he hopped into action.

"Summer?! What's taking so long doll?"

I massaged my temples with my fingers. "Oh my God. This is a nightmare."

"Come on." He gestured with his head while buttoning his pants. "I'm dressed. Let her in."

I stood there for a moment, my eye moving from him to the door and back again.

"Summer, come on." Jayce secured the final button on his dress shirt. "Open the door."

"Doll?" my mother called again from the other side of my door.

"*Ugh*, fine." I folded the flat sheet I snatched off the bed to cover myself, securing the bedding in place around my body. "But say as little as possible to her, do you hear me?"

He snorted a laugh.

"I'm so serious," I shrieked with big eyes.

At the door, as Jayce slipped his foot into his leather loafers, I twisted the knob and opened the door to my mother, dressed in this season's fashions up to the oversized sorbet-orange floppy hat.

"Oh, wow!" she exhaled as Jayce stood with his back straight after pushing his foot into his shoe. "Aren't *you* a tall order of gorgeous?"

He chuckled.

"Mother, Jayce." I gestured to Jayce. "Jayce, this is my mother, Priscilla. Now bye, go."

Jayce laughed this time. He opened the door wider to step through. "It was nice meeting you. Y'all enjoy your Saturday."

Behind my mother's back, Jayce blew me a kiss before heading down the steps.

My mother followed me into my apartment and closed the door.

"Mother, what are you doing here?"

"To shop," she answered. "Don't you remember? One of your neighbors was leaving for a run and was kind enough to let me in to come up. I'm here to accompany you to pick out outfits for your date with the junior partner tonight. We talked about this the day he asked you out, didn't we?"

I slapped my forehead. "Oh, right, that's tonight. I completely forgot about that."

"Figures." She turned to glance and point at the door. "You've got a very handsome distraction to assist with that."

"Mother."

"How did you two become acquainted?" she asked. "His vernacular and deep city accent is a dead give away of where he's from."

I whipped my head in her direction. "He's an intern competing for the same position I'm vying for at *Brown, Bloom & Associates.*"

"Really?!" She pressed her hand to her chest. "How on earth did *he* secure an internship at the firm?"

"Jayce is actually very smart, mother."

"Doll..." She shook her head. "Please don't let good sex cloud your judgment."

"Mother, please." I sat on the couch a few feet away from my bed. The same bed where Jayce blew my mind yet again the night before.

"That internship is yours so you can have a little fun in the meantime, but don't you lose your focus, and certainly not on that one."

I stared at her.

"You understand that the two of you can never date seriously, right? Just do whatever it is you two are doing, with protection of course. I hope you're using protection, Summer. Oh, you know what, please! Be a doll and spare me the details. I adore our relationship and appreciate how open you are with me, but I have my limits."

"Yes, mother, we use protection. I'm no fool." I chuckled. "And Jayce and I are just hanging out, he knows that. But lately... I don't know."

"*Please know* and know with some sense." She parked herself beside me. "Keep in mind when you date and marry a man, you are dating and marrying his family. Yes, this one may be smart, but are the rest of his kinfolk? Probably not."

I twisted my lips to one side.

"He might be an anomaly."

A part of me knew she was right. Something beyond my realm of understanding was pulling me to him though. I couldn't figure out what it was.

"Anton is a better catch, so please..." She pressed her hand to my shoulder to nudge me up. "Go freshen up so we can head over to Georginas! I booked an appointment and you're aware of how much I hate being late. She's got some pieces already picked out for you and champagne sitting on ice for the both of us. I cannot wait to see you in them. Anton will adore you tonight if I have any say in it."

I forced a smile and stood to my feet, hoping that after my shower I could get Jayce off my body and my mind so I could focus on Anton, the *real* catch.

So much for that...

I warmed a seat in a crowded rooftop lounge and restaurant, *Blyss*, listening to Anton blab on and on about... something. I'd tuned him out after he began talking about the summer home he was considering buying before the end of the season. That was after he carried on a monologue about moving up in the company. He gave no opportunity for me to pose questions or chime in. Anton just kept vomiting details all over me about himself.

I arrived for our date an hour ago. He had me waiting outside the establishment for well over half-an-hour. He blamed traffic, but I took a similar route, and traffic was very light.

"I've got my eyes on the new class *Mercedes Benz*," he remarked through bites. "They say the wheels glide like silverware over butter on the road."

I smiled and nodded, just like mother taught me. My eyes roamed around me, taking in the lights of the surrounding skyscrapers glittering in the night. Voices hummed around us and utensils scraped against china while glasses clinked too. I tried to focus on everything except for the man sitting across from me. Not that he even noticed. Anton was too busy discussing what I came to realize was his favorite subject - him.

The truth was, I was drowning in this date. I hadn't spoken one word because Anton did most of the talking. All topics I tried to switch to, he redirected with more unsolicited conversation about himself.

Anton was handsome though. So very handsome.

He wore a crisp black suit with debonair leather loafers. They tailored his outfit to perfection, his haircut and goatee shaped like he'd stepped off a *Calvin Klein* photo shoot before arriving for our date. He was great eye candy, decadent in every way. But Anton was too much treat for me. I found myself starved for soul food.

There I was, occupying the seat across from a man with the credentials and background I pictured the man of my dreams having, and he was a sitting nightmare to keep company with. I was staring right at a manifestation fail. In that instance, I really wished I didn't get what I thought I wanted.

"So, let me ask you something," he voiced.

I perked up in my seat.

Okay, an opportunity to share something about me. Maybe this date is salvageable after all!

He pulled out his phone and tapped around before switching the screen to face me. "What do you think of this car for me?"

My eyelids fluttered closed, and I fought the grimace that threatened to morph my face. "It's perfect. I love the color."

"Right!" he beamed. "I have two other cars in my garage in the Hampton's. This would make an excellent inclusion."

"I grew up in the Hampton's," I offered. "My mother is still a resident."

"Hmph, that's nice Summer." He took a sip of his drink and focused elsewhere.

I stared at him for a moment before dropping my view on my food. As I pushed around the small bits of Kobe beef on my gold-rimmed china, I wondered what Jayce was up to. If he was thinking about me, too. Instantly, my mind flashed back to the night before. What he did to me, how he made me feel.

A strong chill crawled down my back as I reminisced about Jayce and I. His mouth on me, hands caressing spots I didn't know could bring so much pleasure when touched. Just the thought made me shiver in my seat.

"Are you cold?" Anton asked across from me.

"The opposite." I grinned. "But, I'm fine."

"How's interning going?"

My brows rose from his interest.

"Great!" I replied. "I'm always excited to start my day at the office."

"Your mother is good friends with a few of the partners and Clyde, the director of human resources. He and I hang out from time to time and he confirmed you're a shoe in."

My smile couldn't be contained on my lips.

"All you have to do is show up, Summer, and the job is yours. I'm sure you've heard that already."

"I did."

"Not that you plan to be there long, right?"

I cocked a brow. "I'm sorry?"

"You know..." He cleaned his mouth with his napkin. "After you find the right man, hopefully me." He smiled. "And marriage becomes the topic, babies would come next and there's no way you'll be able to work *and* be a good mother."

My jaw dropped.

"Definitely go to law school. Education is of value to parent. You must have excellent reading and comprehension skills to fill out pediatric forms, so a fine school is important."

I gagged.

"But, I doubt you'll want to have a career outside of being a mother. Stay-at-home mom will suit you better."

The waiter servicing our table was retracing his steps to a neighboring table when I grabbed his forearm to get his attention. "Can I *please* have a shot of whiskey?" I paid Anton a glance, then grabbed the waiter's forearm tighter. "Make it two shots."

"Right away," the waiter responded, breaking free from my grip.

"Strong drink," Anton quipped across from me. "Are you not enjoying the bottle of Shiraz I ordered? It's the best here."

The waiter returned with my favorite spirit quick fast and before he could sit the second glass of whiskey on the table, I took it out of his hand.

"The wine is cute, but I will need whiskey to survive the rest of this date," I admitted, answering Anton's question. I smiled politely before downing the brown beverage in one smooth gulp.

"Survive the rest of this date?" he repeated. "What's that supposed to mean?"

"Please tell me you're kidding." I asserted. "All we've spoken about is you."

"It's a date," he retorted.

"Yes, a *date*. The goal should have been to learn about one another. You've asked me nothing about me."

"You have asked nothing about me either."

"That's because you've been taking up all the air in the room, talking so much about yourself I couldn't squeeze in even a word with you." I lifted the second glass and sipped it this time. The date was terrible, but my plan wasn't to get wasted and *Blyss* did not add a drop of water to their drinks, I discovered.

"No other woman has ever complained until you."

"Relevance?" I challenged without blinking an eye.

He dropped his fork into his plate and cleaned his lips once again. "I'm a catch!"

"Oh *you're* something."

"I'm a junior partner before thirty, own a condo in the city, and a home in East Hampton..."

"Yes, yes," I cut in. "We covered all of that within the first fifteen minutes of being seated at our table. Before the food even arrived, actually."

That's when it hit me... I was on a date with myself. Anton was... me. This was exactly what I did, discuss myself to the annoyance of others.

Oh. God!

I took a bigger sip of my drink when that realization settled in.

"You know what?" He pushed his chair back and pulled out his wallet from his back pocket, dropping two one hundred-dollar bills onto the table. "I'm heading out. Are you fine getting home alone?"

I peered up at him in shock.

He wasn't even going to see me home?!

Instead of answering, I tossed the rest of my drink back and stood up too. My eyes burned into him before I turned and simply walked away from the table. No words were left to speak. The date was a disaster, and now I'd have to answer to my mother.

"I wonder what Jayce is up to," I mused as I exited the restaurant.

Fourteen

JAYCE

"I like your place," Veronika complimented the moment she found comfort in her spot on my floor.

We lounged on my black area rug in my living room, which shared the space with my bedroom.

"Thanks," I replied. "I appreciate it. I keep everything in here real simple as you can see."

Her eyes roamed around the layout, falling on my black leather couch and matching armchair. Her view skated over the area rug headed for my bedroom. My floor plan was minimal. One night table, a lamp, a few feet away, a hamper with a basketball hoop hovering over the basket of clothes. I didn't keep the usual headboard nailed to my bed like most people. Instead, I built a bookcase in that spot to hold my books so it could be at arm's reach.

"You have a lot of black history textbooks and law books on your bookcase headboard." She smiled. "You read a lot?"

"Absolutely." I flipped open my spiraled notebook. "Gotta keep the mind sharp."

She licked her lips and resumed scoping out the place.

I pointed my attention down on the college ruled lines in my notebook and positioned my ballpoint pen to write, more than prepared to set up the outline for our assignment. Jeff assigned us a new task the day before. Veronika offered to stop by, but I'd headed straight to Summer's after work instead. So, Roni opted to come by on a Saturday night, which was tonight.

"Is that your family?" she asked, pointing at my coffee table where I kept two dollar-store picture frames. In one was a picture of my mother, two siblings, and I on the Coney Island boardwalk. The other frame held a photo of my father sitting on a bench in our project.

"Yup," I replied.

"You look just like your dad."

"That's what people tell me." My attention was down on my notebook as I began scribbling prospective ideas. When Veronika offered to visit my place, I wanted to turn her down but didn't see the need to. She was single, I was single. If something popped off between us, there would be no one to answer to.

Not exactly.

Besides, I was more focused on getting work done, anyway.

"He must have been extremely handsome in his youth."

I turned my head slowly to peer over at her. And when I did, I noticed the top three buttons undone on her black buttoned-blouse. The top curve of her breasts peeked out. I peeled my eyes away from the mini peepshow to make eye contact with her again.

I said, "That's what people say too."

"Can I be honest with you?" Her voice dropped a few octaves, and I already knew what time it was.

"Yeah." I closed my notebook. "What's up?"

"I didn't really come over here to compose mock questions for the pseudo-trial Jeff is making us do on Monday."

My eyes drifted down to her cleavage again. "So, what did you come over here for, Roni?"

"I *love* when you call me Roni."

Not a second later, Veronika jumped me, attacking me with a kiss. Her mouth was warm against mine, her tiny hands moving all over me.

"Roni!" I mumbled on her lips, but shorty was well underway to getting what she wanted.

She straddled me. Slid her hands down my chest and was traveling south, her destination my dick.

"God, your chest is so muscular," she breathed on my lips. "Your whole body..." She palmed my dick hard, and I flinched from the unintentional pain. "You are so unbelievably sexy and blessed!"

"Veronika," I tried again.

"*Shh*," she shushed on my lips, damn near tearing my shirt off me. "You said you liked bold women, right?" Veronika ripped her blouse opened. The remaining fastened buttons popped off and bounced along my hardwood floor and off the area rug, scattering everywhere. "Well..." She grabbed my hands and placed them on each breast. "... here I am."

I snatched my hands off them and grabbed her by the shoulders.

"Veronika!" I yelled, pushing her back a little. "Stop."

We made eye contact, and I witnessed how the smile previously on her lips melted away

"I did *not* plan for us to do this tonight." I pointed at my notebook. "I really wanted to draft these questions so we're prepared for Monday."

"What?!"

"Look, you're beautiful." I grabbed her by the waist and lifted her off me. Getting the hint, she moved over to my side, clutching the sides of her blouse together, covering herself. "But we have to focus..."

"Do you tell *Summer* this?"

The way Veronika snarled Summer's name, dragging out each syllable like her name was a medical term for some disease, made me lower my head and scrub my brows with my fingertips.

"*Oh, yes,* I figured it out. I know the two of you are fucking and fucking a lot. It's written all over her face and yours." She scoffed. "The two of you can barely pay attention when around each other. So I find it ironic tonight, *with me*, you want to focus on the assignment at hand."

She had a point there, but I hadn't planned to get into that or to explain myself.

"So typical," she continued, leaning back against my couch and crossing her arms. "You guys always go for the light and bright ones with hair extending down their backs. Meanwhile, us chocolate sisters are left waiting in the wind as usual."

I turned to face her. "First, Veronika you are gorgeous."

She kissed her teeth. "Yeah, right."

I grabbed her by the chin, pivoted her head to face me, stared her in her eyes, and said, "Yeah. Right."

A smile pulled at her lips.

"My mother and baby sister are chocolate sisters as you say, and they are absolutely exquisite too. My first love, someone who I loved very much, was darker than you. So, beautiful, please understand when I tell you I do not prefer light and bright as you've claimed."

"So, then what is it about Summer that's got you so hooked like this? To the point where I'm here in your face and you want to be loyal to *her*? *That* girl?! You don't have me fooled with all this *you want to focus* bullshit."

"I *do* want to focus," I defended.

She pursed her lips and tilted her head to the side.

I chuckled. "Okay maybe not *that* much."

"So?" she pushed.

"I've known Summer for a really long time," I began. "She's impossible as you put it but the connection we have is cosmic."

"Cosmic? With *her*? How?!" Her jaw dropped. "Are we even talking about the same person? All Summer talks about is herself. She's a modern day *Narcissus*. I bet she'd drown herself in her own reflection if she could."

I shrugged my lips. Veronika was absolutely right.

"Is the sex that good with her?"

"Do you want me to answer honestly?"

"Wow." She leaned against the couch behind us. "It *is* that good, huh?"

"Our thing started off that way," I clarified. "Only being about sex. But now... I don't know."

That was the first time I admitted it out loud. The realization that this thing between Summer and I was becoming something more than physical. It was my first time admitting it to myself, or anyone for that matter. Being honest felt... right.

"Lucky *bitch*," Veronika mumbled to herself. She turned to her left and started gathering her stuff together.

"What's up? What are you doing?"

"Leaving." She pushed her books into her messenger bag.

"We haven't even brainstormed the questions yet!"

"Draft the questions alone," she spat. "Or call Summer to help you out. Frankly, I don't give a shit."

Veronika stood to her feet.

"Oh, come on!"

"Maybe," she added as she made her way around my coffee table, her shirt falling open, her B-cup breasts in full view. "After she stops by, you two can fuck before you complete any work. Or don't get any work done for all I care. That way, the permanent position at the firm and the bonus is mine. I'm out of here."

I pushed myself up on my feet to stand up. "Are you serious right now?"

Veronika turned to face me. "Fuck you, Jayce!"

My jaw dropped. "Yoooo! What's wrong with you?"

She said nothing in response, only barreled out my apartment and slammed the door behind herself as she left.

I threw my hands up in the air. "What the fuck was that?!"

My phone ringing on my coffee table stole my attention next. I walked over to the device to see Summer's name lit up on the screen. Shock melted away from the spectacle that happened a moment ago and instantly was replaced with joy. I ran my palm down my face, trying to wipe away the new feeling Summer caused by me simply reading her name.

"What is this girl doing to me, man?" I asked myself right before answering.

"Ms. Summer McKoy," I said into the phone.

She giggled. "Mr. Jayce Martin."

"Nah." I smiled. "My name don't got that gleam the way yours does."

"Well, can't argue with that."

I laughed.

"What are you up to?" she quizzed.

"Oh, nothing." I walked to my king-sized bed and dropped myself backwards onto the mattress. "Just had the study date from hell."

"I doubt your date from hell compares to the shitty date I had with Anton."

"That was tonight?"

"Yes, it was." She exhaled sharply. "My mother visited the city to accompany me shopping just for this date, and it was awful. Now I have to figure out a way to tell her."

I turned on my side. "I thought he was the perfect find."

Even through the phone, I could sense her rolling her eyes at me from the way she sighed.

"He reminded me of... *me*."

I bursted into laughter, holding my gut. "And what? You don't like you?"

"It's not that," she purred. Her voice was amazing over the phone. Made me want to leave my place barefoot and walk crosstown to her apartment just to hear it in person.

"It was too *much*," she added. "He didn't even try to learn anything about me. Then the discussion turned to our future, *I think*, and he switched into this sexist pompous jackass who became repulsive the longer I remained in his company."

"Well, that's not you at all, Summer," I admitted.

"You mean that? Because I think there are people who would disagree with you. In fact, I *know* they would."

My brow arched. This was the vulnerability I spoke about. A vulnerability that peeked out when I least expected. Made her more appealing, sexier, and made me want her more than physically.

"Let me take you out on a date."

"Wh-what?!"

"Anywhere you want to go. I'll show you how a real man handles a woman like you."

She chuckled a little and sounded so cute. "Oh, okay, sure. Umm... there's this great Italian restaurant that opened last month in the meatpacking district. The entrée's are kind of expensive though..."

"Then that's where we're going."

Silence fell over the line.

"Are you still here with me, Ms. McKoy?"

She moaned. "Do not say that. Reminds me of last night when you asked me the same thing while we... you know."

I bit my lip, thinking back. Summer was a boss, had boss tendencies, confidence through the roof. In bed, though? She was innocent, submissive, a little unsure but didn't mind me taking the lead, and straight dominating her. That shit was a total turn on. It was like our little secret and I was slowly getting to the point where I didn't want her to share that part of herself with anyone else but me.

Did I just think that?

"I could come over and give you another round," I offered.

She laughed. "No, I'm beat, and drunk."

"Summer," I scolded.

"I needed a drink after the shit I experienced with Anton. The whiskey at the restaurant was okay, but it was a requirement that I crack open the bottle in my cabinet to keep from jumping out of my window."

"You're so dramatic." I snickered. "Well, I'm gonna fix that for you, don't you worry."

Silence again, and I knew why.

"Are you smiling, Ms. McKoy?"

"Mm-hmm."

"Kills me I can't witness it in person."

She giggled. "Goodnight, Jayce."

"Goodnight, beautiful."

FIFTEEN

Two weeks later, post my date with Anton, I relaxed across from Jayce in *Sunny's Italiano.*

The new restaurant, only a few weeks old, bustled with energy. It wasn't loud, or anything like that, just packed. But somehow, Jayce reserved us a table away from the crowd and at a corner window near the back of the restaurant.

"I know somebody who knows somebody who washes dishes in the back." He smiled when we took our seats. "They promised to hook me up."

And that they did.

The space was charming. Individual tiny square tables, gorgeous sconce lights hung overhead. Tall cylinder votive candle holders kept small tea light candles contained while they floated on water.

The atmosphere was romantic, adding to how appetizing Jayce appeared that night. He wore a simple button-down black shirt with the matching trousers. His narrowed-toe toffee-colored loafers shined just as much as his freshly cut fade. We couldn't keep our eyes off each other.

For the night, I kept it simple, throwing on a basic taupe-colored low neck midi-dress paired with pink velvet chunky heeled sandals.

I wanted to jump his bones so badly or him jump mine. Jayce liked to take control, and I let him because he was so damn good at it. No instruction or guidance needed. I could actually lay back and come, hard, with him.

"So, what do you want to have?" he asked, dropping his eyes down to his menu.

"Oh, that's right," I replied. "We have to eat."

He laughed, glancing up at me. "I mean, you know... it *is* a restaurant."

I smiled.

"There it goes." He smiled back.

I shyly shifted my eyes off him, dropping my view to my menu.

We ordered our food and when our dishes arrived, Jayce and I dived in.

He chose the penne a la vodka, and I opted for the shrimp parmesan linguine.

Not much talking happened that night at the restaurant between us. Jayce communicated with me nonverbally and I did the same.

We exchanged smiles. Winks on his part. Jayce and I licked our lips and gawked at what we could see above our meals. His foot tapped mine beneath the table to regain my attention, and I rubbed the toe of my shoes against his calves. Our eyes were partially shaded in low lids, his tongue slowly swiping his bottom lip.

It was like that until we were a few bites away from cleaning our plates, and I heard a familiar voice from several tables away.

My father's voice to be precise.

I didn't hear it often. The last time my father and I had a proper conversation was when he stopped by my mother's Hampton's mansion for my ninth birthday party. His voice was husky with an old New York swag. He still enunciated *coffee* as if there were an "a" hidden in the "o" of the word.

"Oh my God," I whispered to myself, loud enough for Jayce to hear.

My eyes searched the surrounding faces until they landed on my father. He wore a tailored gray suit, a three-piece. His jacket hung behind his chair while his gray vest and white shirt with the matching gray tie were in full-view.

"My father is here," I confirmed standing to my feet. "I'll be right back."

"Aight," Jayce said as I walked away.

I couldn't get to my father's table fast enough. My cheeks were already hurting from how hard I smiled on my way over to him.

I was feet away when I noticed the two girls that crowded him. They resembled him. They had to be my sisters.

I'd never met them. My mother revealed that his wife never approved of us all meeting. Apparently, my mother and father had a short relationship before he left my mother for his now wife. Him marrying his wife and starting a family of their own crushed my mother and was one reason she's never really gotten over their breakup to date again. Mother transmuted her heartbreak by spending most of her time and energy grooming me and planning my future.

"Dad?" I asked just two steps away from the table.

His smoky grays rose to meet my eyes. The smile that once plastered his lips slowly dissipated.

"Su-Summer," my father, *the* Steven McKoy, stuttered. "Wh—? What are you doing here?"

I turned to point at the table where Jayce and I were seated to see him staring back at us. "I'm out with a friend."

My eyes focused on one of the girls. They shared the same light colored gray eyes as my father. Both of the girls did, actually. They had to be only 18 and 19-years-old. One's hair was short, just above her ears while the other one, the one giving me the meanest glare, had long dark super straight hair. I knew it had to be a superb flat-ironing job. My father was biracial, but was more on the lighter side of the spectrum, à la Steph Curry.

"Hi," I said to the one with the longest hair. "I'm—"

"I know who you are," she spat, leaning back in her chair.

"Deja," my father said.

"No, dad." She twisted her head at our father, and he glanced away. Her eyes returned on me. "The nerve of you to approach our table."

"I'm sorry?"

"Yes, you *are* sorry," the other chimed in. "This is a family dinner. What can *we* help you with?"

I jerked my head back. "Look, I just saw my father over here and I thought—"

"You thought wrong," Deja spat back. "Destini, look," she called to the other girl, "she has her mother's face."

"I know," Destini said next. "How tragic."

"Girls!" my father spoke up.

I wrinkled my brows as I took one step back. My eyes met with my father's and he shut his lids and pushed all the air he had in him out of his nose.

"Summer," Jayce said behind me.

I turned to see him standing only feet away, and I wanted to collapse right there. The muscles in my stomach twisted, and my throat spasmed. The food I'd eaten only moments ago threatened to reappear all over the white tablecloth draped on my father and siblings' table.

"Come on, babe." I felt Jayce's hands on either side of my shoulders, gently pulling me away, but I wouldn't move.

"Summer," my father spoke again, "go with your friend."

I inhaled sharply, taking one final look at my father. Not able to take another second of the somberness in his eyes, I turned away quickly, pushing past Jayce to return to our table to grab my purse. The tears threatened to fall, but I held them back as I damn near ran out of the restaurant.

———

The cab ride back to my apartment was quiet. Jayce didn't ask me anything, and I didn't volunteer information either. My heart hammered in my chest, competing with my pulse. In a matter of seconds, my world had come crashing down and I couldn't understand why.

Once we arrived, I stormed through my apartment's door, briefly bending forward to unstrap my heels half the way inside, then headed straight to my kitchen's cabinet.

I slammed the bottle of whiskey down on the counter, pulled out a crystalline double old fashioned glass from the same cabinet, then snatched open my freezer to thumb out two ice cubes.

The brown liquid tumbled out the bottle and fell into the glass, which I lifted to my lips and tossed back. Did that twice more until I abandoned the glass and drank straight from the bottle's spout.

"Summer," Jayce said at my kitchen's entrance. I'd forgotten he was even there.

He had the most sympathetic expression on his face when I twisted my head to glare his way.

I had to laugh at myself as I turned to face him. The bottle's spout was to my lips when I took another swig of whiskey.

"I bet you think real highly of me now."

Jayce dropped his head a little to scratch the back of his ear.

"They treated me like I was some beast from a lagoon. Can you believe that? Me. They treated *me* like that."

He stood there, his eyes soft and fixed on me.

"Everything I have ever done was for *his* approval. Run for class president because my mother said he would be so proud. Practice ballet because my mother promised he'd sit in the audience of every one of my recitals. Compete for a law internship at one of the most prestigious law firms in the country because my mother swore it would impress my father." The tears began to fall before I could stop them.

Jayce took steps toward me, but I held a hand up to stop him before he got too close. "No, *please*, no." I shook my head. "I need to *feel* this. I have to drown in it. Lose my breath in the fact that my father wants nothing to do with me."

Jayce ran his hand down his face slow.

"Deal with the reality that the one man I worked hard to fall in love with me, hates me. That my sisters despise me."

"Summer—"

"Shut up!" I yelled, pushing him back twice until he stepped away. "I don't want you to pet me like a dog with your words right now, Jayce."

The spout was to my lips again as I chugged the whiskey this time. The spirit burned all the way down to my stomach as I gulped. Jayce took giant steps toward me and snatched the bottle out of my hand, spilling a little of the whiskey to the floor.

"Give it back!"

"No!" he yelled. He turned to the sink and emptied the rest down the drain.

"Why the fuck did you do that?!" I asked while grabbing for his arm to stop him.

"Because you don't need it, Summer." His eyes bored into me as he emptied the last remnants down the drain. "You've had enough."

"*I'll* never be enough."

Jayce slammed the now empty bottle on the counter and turned to face me. "What did you say?"

My bottom lip trembled. I closed my eyes and swallowed hard to gain some composure. What I said was what I've always felt but never could fix my lips to admit it, not even to myself.

"I'm not enough," I whispered.

He shook his head slow. "Summer."

"Everything I tried I quit because I saw it didn't do the job of getting him to show up. To just *show up* for me. I never really liked anything my mother signed me up for. Soccer, gymnastics, pageants. I finally fell in love with ballet... but then she made it about him, saying that if I continued to perform as well as I was performing, he would show up at every one of my recitals, but he never did. So I put my love for it to the back of my mind and started seriously practicing." I bobbled my head. "But no longer for the love or enjoyment of dancing. I practiced *for him,* because the better I was at it, he'd have to attend a show to see for himself, right?

"Then, in my last year of high school, when I landed the coveted roles of all roles at my dance studio, one of the most acclaimed studios in New York, he still didn't show up. So I quit." I shrugged my shoulders. "My mother continues to insist my father would be so proud if I do the things she says for me to do, the most recent thing this internship, but it's clear now that none of it will ever matter. It never did."

Jayce walked up to me and ran his thumbs along my cheeks.

"When I was 10-years-old I convinced myself he would show up for my solo act once I became a big girl. When I was 21-years-old, I filled out the application to intern at *Brown, Bloom & Associates* and told myself he'd be so proud once I landed that one sought after position."

Jayce stared at me, waiting for me to continue.

"I was today-years-old when I realized that no matter what I do, regardless of how hard I work, despite how phenomenal *I* think *I* am, my father will never show up because I'll *never* be enough for him. I'm just *so* tired of trying to prove something that isn't true."

Jayce lowered his forehead to mine and held it there. "I don't wanna ever hear you say that again... *ever*. Your worth is never measured by someone else. This thing beating right here is your scale," he said, tapping the space where my heart ached. "You're enough, you understand me?"

Like a levy, tears bursted from my eyes and my wails sounded next. Jayce pulled me close to him and held me tight, allowing me to cry against him.

In his arms, I felt safe, comforted. I'd spilled the one thing that has haunted me for years. The only ugly truth I'd been in denial about from the time I was old enough to reason - my father's rejection.

Jayce bent his legs at the knees to lift me up and off my feet. He carried me to my bed and removed my dress.

That man kissed me like he'd never kissed me before. Caressed my skin like it was the most delicate thing he's ever touched.

"You are enough. You're more than enough," he whispered against my lips and I melted into a puddle of emotions.

I moved my hand to the crotch of his pants when he stopped me.

"Jayce," I begged.

"Nah, Summer." He balanced himself on his forearm and hovered over me while shaking his head. "You've had too much to drink—"

"Please don't deny me too, Jayce," I said back, voice breaking.

He swallowed hard, then looked away. I turned his head, so he'd focus on me again, then pulled his face to mine. My tongue cloaked in whiskey slid into his mouth and he allowed it. I lifted from my position below him, and he turned with me. Seated on top of him, I unsnapped my bra from the front and watched his lids grow heavy the moment he saw my breasts spill out.

Gently, I undid the button of his shirt one by one. His hands cupped my breasts before he outlined the curve of my waist to grab my ass.

Finally naked, Jayce upright, his back against my headboard, I slid down the length of his torso until I was face to face with his hard-on. I refused to break focus on him as I wrapped my lips around his staff. His head slowly slung back, and a groan escaped his slacked jaw. He buried his hands in my hair, holding my strands at the roots as I bobbed up and down on him.

"Damn, Summer," he groaned at the ceiling as the head of his dick mushroomed between the roof of my mouth and the bed of my tongue.

A few moments of that, his dick finally spasmed, twice, signaling he was close when he gently pulled me off him and whispered, "Come here beautiful."

"But—"

"I want you close to me for that part."

Without further protest, I crawled to him as he grabbed a condom. After positioning myself astride his hips, I balanced myself on my knees, and lowered down on him inch by inch.

Once I found my rhythm, I rolled my hips on top of him, slid back and forth against his lap. He filled me, left no room for nothing else. He kept his hands on my derrière as I moved back and forth over him. Jayce leaned his head even further back and closed his eyes when the swivel of my hips took us to another place.

"Fuck, Summer," he whispered, his hands still gripping my ass, eyes still shut. "Yes, baby. Just like that."

Our moans matched as I rode myself to the peak of my release.

I sunk my fingertips into his shoulders when my body trembled and I'd lost my flow distracted by coming.

"I got you love. I got you." Jayce grabbed me by the thighs and leaned me back to change positions.

He was on top of me now, pumping in and out. Jayce moved like he owned the blueprint to my body. Like he'd mastered finding its sweet spots in the short time we'd been intimate. He'd memorized my pleasure map while discovering and creating my new weaknesses for him. I watched him watch me until my vision blurred from my eyes rolling. For a moment, only a moment, things were perfect. Jayce stroked me with skill, transporting me mentally to another plane where all that mattered was him and I, and the pleasure he conjured up between us.

I met my climax head on, rocking beneath him.

I laid there, coming, my orgasm feeling like it would burst through me and last forever. Right at the moment where breathing became an afterthought, and I believed I'd lose consciousness, he whispered in my ear, "Know that you're enough for me."

Sixteen

JAYCE

"I should leave," I thought to myself as I waited outside of *McKoy Enterprises*. It was easy to find *M.E.* just by googling Summer's father, Steven McKoy, online.

I didn't like the way she looked yesterday afternoon when I finally peeled myself away from her to head back home. And at nine in the morning, here I stood in front of *M.E.'s* tall glass building waiting for Steven to arrive.

I'd spoken to his receptionist as soon as I stepped through the office suite's door an hour prior. Gave her some bullshit excuse about writing a paper on him for my summer course for graduate school. It was the first thing I could think to tell her. She confirmed his usual arrival time was 9 a.m. I needed to be on the other side of town by 10:30 a.m. for my internship, so the time was perfect so long as he actually arrived on time.

"What the fuck am I doing?" I asked myself.

That's what Summer did to me these days, made me do things I couldn't believe I was doing when I did them. Showing up at her father's job to confront him for hurting her feelings made the top of the list.

I dropped my head into my hands and inhaled a deep breath.

When I lifted my eyes out my hands, I spotted Steven stepping out of a shiny silver *Rolls Royce*, shaking hands with another gentleman dressed in a nice suit.

"I'll call you when I get upstairs and we can run the numbers, Todd."

The man nodded his understanding. "Thanks for breakfast."

A woman, young with brown skin and hair just two shades lighter than her skin tone, followed behind Steven.

"Uh, Mr. McKoy," I called as he passed me.

He turned his head in my direction and when his light gray eyes settled on me, he paused in step.

"Um, I apologize for just showing up like this, but I'm a friend of Summer's—"

"Yes." He adjusted his tie's direction. "I know who you are. You were with her Saturday night."

"Ye-Yeah." My eyes moved to the woman standing behind him, and he followed my line of vision. "Do you mind if I speak with you privately, Mr. McKoy, sir?"

"Of course." He gestured with his head. "Let's head into my office."

Steven pointed his attention at the woman. "Maia, please clear my schedule for the next 15-minutes. Just let me know when Mr. Wellington arrives. I want to be on time for that meeting."

He tapped my shoulder and angled his chin toward the turnstile doors. "Let's go, son."

I followed Mr. McKoy through the building owned by him. A large poster-sized photo of him dressed to the nines graced the lobby along with photos of him with some of the most famous celebrities known to even people who lived in huts in third world countries.

"How's Summer?" he asked as we stepped on to the elevator.

Even the elevator sparkled from the chromed doors to the polished floors.

"I'm sure she's had better days," I answered.

After what felt like only seconds, the elevator opened to his office that offered a dope view of the city.

"Wow," I breathed.

He chuckled as he made his way around his desk. "Impressive isn't it?"

"Beyond that."

Everything appeared different from the top floor of the high-rise. I briefly marveled at the tops of skyscrapers with heights I believed extended inches below the sky. Well, at least they seemed that way from my view on the sidewalk. My eyes roamed around me, falling on the large office desk that may as well had come with its own sparkle chime because the shit gleamed.

"Have a seat over here." He pointed at the armchair opposite his desk.

"Thanks," I replied, taking the seat.

"So..." He unbuttoned his tailored navy blue blazer and took a seat in the leather chair behind his desk. "What brings you here?"

I ran my hands down my face slow and shook my head. "Man, I have no idea *what* I'm doing here to be honest."

Steven smiled. "You're here for her."

My eyes connected with his.

"I take it Summer is upset."

"Rightly so and beyond words, sir."

He exhaled through his mouth. "It's complicated... Summer's mother, Priscilla, and my relationship."

"How complicated could it be that you wouldn't be in your daughter's life?"

Steven furrowed his brows.

"With all due respect, sir," I added.

"I like you for her." He nodded. "You're forward, protective. Good. She'll need a man like you in her life."

She needs you, was what I wanted to say, but instead I kept my mouth closed and my ears opened, waiting for the real response.

"The complicated that almost ended my marriage when my wife found out about it." He blew his exhale through his lips. "Also the complicated that when I was having the affair, I had no knowledge that Summer was being made."

My eyes widened. "What do you mean by that?"

Steven scratched the back of his head.

"Are you saying Summer's mother was your side chick who trapped you with Summer?!"

Steven chuckled. "We didn't quite call women like Summer's mother side chicks in my day. And I'm not sure if Priscilla ever *trapped* me, she just got pregnant by me without me knowing—"

He cut his words short to shake his head. "Son, under no circumstances can what we discuss here leave this room. Do you understand?"

I folded my lips into my mouth and nodded.

"Summer has lived a wonderful life, I've seen to it. Insisted that she take my last name because she was my firstborn. At the beginning, I didn't want Summer's mother, Priscilla, to carry out the pregnancy. I knew what it would do to my marriage, but Priscilla refused to do anything but have her baby, and she raised an awe-inspiring young woman I'm proud to have bearing my name."

"If you feel that way..." I scooted to the edge of my seat. "Why don't you see her? She feels rejected."

"And I'm sorry about that, really I am, but my marriage, my immediate family... they come first."

I wrinkled my brows.

"I would have loved to have a relationship with Summer but what I did to my wife, stepping out of our marriage, was wrong. And for that reason, my wife forbade me from being involved with Summer in any way. Priscilla used to call often, my office only, but then my wife got wind of it and gave me an ultimatum to cut all ties with Priscilla or she would leave."

The words coming out of his mouth weighed heavy on me, making me sink in my seat. I reclined back, scrubbing my brows. The truth was, I didn't come all this way for any of this or to learn this side of Summer. I just wanted to tell her father how fucked up he was for making her cry. Learning all that other shit during my visit took me back.

"I put them in a gorgeous home in East Hampton, made sure Priscilla had the finest for herself and our daughter. Enrolled Summer in the best schools throughout her academic career and she has flourished beyond my wildest dreams, but I can only watch from afar. I hate to admit that, but..." He shrugged. "It's the ugly truth."

"Whoa." I blew raspberries with my lips. "I don't understand why you're telling me any of this. I didn't really come here for—"

"Because you're good for her," he told me.

"Summer and I," I began, "we're not serious. We're not even in a relationship—"

"That's clear." He smiled. "She referred to you as her *friend*. But you showing up at my corporate office not understanding why you cared so much to do so tells me otherwise. Just because you haven't admitted what you are to each other, to yourself, doesn't mean there isn't something there."

"Mr. McKoy," a voice echoed from his phone on his desk, "your 9:30 is on his way up."

"Thanks Maia." Steven pushed his chair back. "Son..."

"Yeah." I jumped to my feet. "Thanks for sitting with me."

"No, thank you." Steven held his hand out and I accepted it. He squeezed my hand a bit in our handshake but never broke eye contact. "And please, lets keep this conversation between the two of us, yes?"

I swallowed hard and nodded.

As I made my way out of his office building and onto the humid city street, I ran my hand from my forehead down over my lips.

"Damn, Summer," I whispered to myself. "Why didn't you tell me?"

SEVENTEEN

SUMMER

I wiggled my toes in the warm sudsy foot tub, watching as translucent pink bubbles popped against my feet.

My mother and I lazed outside in her gazebo, receiving her favorite gel mani and pedi from her on-call manicurists.

"Oh, Allison, make sure you pay special attention to my doll's cuticles. She neglects them now that she's competing in her internship." My mother lifted her eyes to mine and smiled. "How much longer, Summer, until you're awarded the job?"

I giggled. "The internship ends in August, mother, so there's still a lot of time left."

"Hmph." My mother held her hands out in front of her to admire the work her manicurist did on her unpolished nails. "I don't see why they don't put the rest of those kids out of their miseries and just give the job to you already."

"Mother, stop it," I scolded. "They're actually *okay* and very smart. All of them are putting up a good fight. Especially Jayce."

My mother whipped her head in my direction at the mention of Jayce's name.

"What?" I quizzed.

She pointed. "That is the third time you've mentioned that boy's name while sitting out here today."

"Has it been that many times?"

"Probably more," she retorted, with squinted eyes.

I rubbed my lips together and moved my view off her to squint up at the sky.

The sun shined so brightly that afternoon, not a cloud in sight. The dome-shape of the gazebo's roof protected us, though. They constructed the pavilion structure in a way to allow for an enchanting breeze to keep us cool.

"How was your date with Anton Jacobs? You never called to give me the details since you've been so busy."

"It was okay."

"Only *okay*?!" She scoffed. "You get asked out so soon into your internship and by a junior partner no less and the date was just *oh-kay*? Has he called you since then?"

"Not exactly."

"Not exactly?" she challenged. "Not exactly, what?"

"Well... not at all, really."

"Summer!"

"Mother, he was a bore, such a terrible date." I rolled my eyes. "I'm relieved he doesn't make things awkward at the office. We just understand we weren't a good match for each other."

My mother shook her head and exhaled with frustration. "What am I going to do with you?"

The manicurist, Allison, squatted down in front of me to lift my feet out of the bubbling water. "Summer, you've taken excellent care of your feet. I haven't had to use the callus shaver on you at all today."

I smiled with unmatched pride. "Thank you. Surprising since I wear stilettos every day and night as of late."

"Night?" My mother asked. "If you aren't going on dates with Anton, where are you going at night with heels on?"

I closed my eyes, realizing my slip. Biting at the side of my lip, I released it to say, "Jayce and I—"

"Oh *God*!" my mother shrieked. "Please, *no*, Summer. I beg of you doll, no!"

"Mother—"

"What do you *see* in that boy?"

"First, mother." I perked up in my seat. "Jayce is *no* boy, he is definitely all man."

"Ick, spare me," she spat while shaking her head disapprovingly

"And you admitted it yourself, he's gorgeous. But besides that he's smart, articulate—"

"Articulate?! Ha!"

"And he treats me good."

"Summer, doll, uh-uh, enough." She turned to face me. "I did not carry you for nine months, groaned in labor for 27-hours with no epidural, birth you then send you to etiquette school to fall in love with some handsome ghetto trash."

I grimaced. "Ghetto trash?! Jayce is not."

"I don't like the way you're defending him, doll. As if you're... you're... Christ! Are you *in love* with this child?"

"No! Absolutely not." I answered too fast. Way too fast giving myself no opportunity to let her claim sit on my heart.

Was I in love?

I mean, Jayce made me happy whenever he was around. I felt understood, seen. And then there was the sex.

Oh God, the sex.

He was so skilled in bed, things had gotten to the point where I craved him minutes after he left my side. I'd never experienced that kind of satisfaction in my entire sexual life and imagining his sex just going away was scary. The thought of never talking to him again, losing the luxury of having him near. Just the idea of Jayce himself going away. That shit terrified me.

"Are you sure about that?" My mother challenged. "Are you absolutely *sure* you aren't falling for this boy?"

I blinked myself out of my head and replied, "Positive."

The manicurist held my hand in hers and began filing down my nails.

"It's like I said," I started, "Jayce and I are only hanging out. From time-to-time we go out to eat. Nowhere fancy except for once."

Instantly, that Saturday night a week ago faded into memory. I'd consciously restrained myself from mentioning the run-in to her because I knew what happened would crush my mother. Telling her would send her to those girls' doorsteps more than prepared to claw their eyes out and send them to their graves with her casket-shaped nails. My mother was prim and proper, but not when things regarded me. She was like a mama bear ready to maul any and everybody. She'd go to war or jail for killing the person who made so much as one tear fall from my eye.

"Well, stop going out with him," she fumed, slamming her hand down on the arm of her chair. "I forbid it!"

My jaw dropped.

"No hanging out, no coming over to spend time. Most definitely no having *sex* with him. Nothing." She leaned closer to me and stared into my eyes. "Do you understand me?"

"Mother," I pleaded.

"Summer Rain McKoy, do you understand *me*?"

My chest heaved up and down as I ground my teeth together, my eyes fixed on hers.

"Hmmm?" she stressed with an eyebrow arched.

I swallowed hard, then reluctantly nodded.

"I cannot hear a nod nor is it a suitable option for an answer. I need you to acknowledge your understanding out loud," she pushed through her teeth.

"Fine," I said, "I won't see him anymore. Happy?"

"Ecstatic." She smiled her satisfaction this time before turning to face forward. Mother pressed the back of her head to the massage chair's headrest and closed her eyes. "I'm doing you a huge favor, doll. You'll thank me in the future when you're not dealing with his eleven baby mamas. He may have none now, but his breed often do soon enough. They're like rabbits. They multiply faster than you can comb your fingers through your pretty hair."

I rolled my eyes away from her and pouted as I pressed my back to my chair.

"And stop your pouting," she ordered next.

I twisted my head against the headrest and in her direction to find her staring right at me. "Pouting causes wrinkles, and you've inherited those prominent laugh lines around your lips from your father. Let's not make them even worse."

"Yes, mother," I mumbled.

"Oh! That reminds me. Allison," she called to the manicurist, "please get Raven on the line. Summer and I could use a facial to go with our new manicures."

I dropped my head back against my chair and closed my eyes, doing my best to fight back my tears, but it was no use. My heart was breaking in my chest into tiny pieces at just the thought of ending things with Jayce.

Eighteen

JAYCE

"Um," Summer questioned beside me. "Where are we?"

Her eyes stared out of my black Toyota Camry's windshield into the dark of the night as she pressed a hand to her chest. Summer kept rubbing the side of her arm, visibly uncomfortable the second we pulled over to the curb. We were in my car and I'd just parked in front of *Stuyvesant Houses*, my first home and where my mother still lived. If I had it my way, she would have been out of here the moment I graduated from *LU*. With only 8K left to come up with, she wouldn't be here for long. Even if my internship didn't pan out the way I expected, I'd figure out a way to get the money. I had to.

"You said you wanted somewhere private and quiet to eat tonight," I answered.

"Yes." She nodded. "And did that request translate to you bringing me to the ghetto?"

I snorted a laugh.

She wasn't being ridiculous. Well, maybe a little. This part of Brooklyn, I'm sure, she only saw in movies. The way she kept her lips tucked in her mouth, I could tell she was freaking out.

"The ghetto?" I parroted. "This is my old neighborhood. I literally just moved out last month."

"Yes, like I said." She twisted her head to glance at me. "The ghetto."

A laugh ripped out my mouth, and she chuckled a little in response.

I didn't take it too hard. I honored all the sides of me, all the experiences I had that shaped me. There was nothing to be ashamed of. This neighborhood played a huge part in making me the man I am today. The good, the bad, and the ugly. Roses grew through concrete out here.

I focused on her again, simply taken by her beauty. For the first time, Summer dressed down. A pair of jeans, a simple black tank top, and rose gold strappy sandals was what she wore for the night. What really had me wanting to turn my car around and take her back to her place to blow her back out was her hair. It was curly, not too tight and not too loose. A comfortable middle. She had it gathered at the crown of her head secured in a bun. Tiny ringlets of curls that escaped her bun fell tousled, framing her heart-shaped face.

"I love your hair like this."

She peeled her eyes away from the passenger side window and gave me a once-over. Her fingers ran down the back of her soft black curls when she shook her head. "It's atrocious. The only reason my hair is this way and not straight is because you called me at the last minute to grab something to eat."

"It's breathtaking."

She blushed. "Jayce, I agreed to come out with you tonight because we need to talk."

"Okay." I shrugged. "Let's talk. Start with telling me why you've been avoiding me at the office for the last few days. What's up with that?"

She shook her head. "This is far from the ideal setting to discuss that."

"All right." I unhooked my seatbelt and unlocked the doors. "Then let's head out."

"What? I-I can't." She glanced through her window again. "I'm wearing *Jimmy Choos* and I've got my *LV* bag on my arm. I can't go out there with this stuff!"

"Baby, everyone in the hood got some *Jimmys* and *LV* merchandise lacing their closets. You're not showing them anything they don't already have, aight? Trust me, you're good. Plus, no one will rob you when you're with me."

She gasped. "And what would happen if I'm not with you?!"

I laughed out loud. "Summer, let's go, love."

Out of the car, Summer walked beside me, her hand clutching the hell out of my hand as we made our way up the path to the building's front door.

The night was dark. A few residents hung out on the green wooden benches in front of their buildings, carrying on conversations with only the light of the street lamps to help them see each other.

"Aye yo, Jayce!" someone called behind me. Automatically I knew who it was from the rasp in their voice. Been hearing it since I was five-years-old when we roamed *Stuyvesant Houses* together as two knuckle-heads. "Aye, what up, D?"

Summer shifted her eyes that way, then did a double take.

"Aw, shit!" Damien hollered into his fist. "Is that my favorite new homie, Ms. Summer?"

She smiled. "Hi, again, Damien."

He pointed at her. "Didn't I tell you he'd be your man?"

She giggled nervously. "He's *not*."

"Yet, Summer. *Yet.*" Damien held up a finger for emphasis.

She laughed this time.

"What y'all out here getting into, anyway?" Damien asked, giving me a pound.

"'Bout to run up here and see what moms is up to."

"Aight, aight." Damien clapped his hands once. "I'm 'bout to get a few rides in. Hit me up if y'all need a lift out of here." He glanced at Summer, rubbing his hands. "Especially if Ms. Summer is tippin'."

She laughed. "I bet. For gas money, right?"

Damien laughed too. "Man, I like you."

"Nah, we drove so we're good, D." I said through my laugh. I gave him a pound. "I'll hit you up either tonight or tomorrow though."

"The way shorty clinging to your arm, I ain't hearing from you tonight," Damien teased and Summer playfully rolled her eyes at him. "I'll holla at you tomorrow."

"No doubt. One." Damien gave me another pound before he walked away and Summer and I continued toward the building.

"It's so interesting how you can switch from one dialect to another," she said close to me.

I smiled at her choice of words.

"Just call me bilingual, baby." I winked.

She giggled while shaking her head.

We'd stopped in front of the box of silver buttons outside the lobby's door when I pressed down on one button to ring my old apartment's bell.

"Shouldn't you have a key?" Summer quizzed. "You said you just moved out."

"I do have a key. I rang the bell to give my mother a heads up that I'm here. I'm courteous like that."

"Hmph," she huffed with a smile.

"Who is it?" my mother's voice echoed from the box's speaker.

"It's me, ma."

The moment we were buzzed in and I pulled opened the lobby's door, the singeing scent of piss smacked us in our faces.

"Oh, Christ!" Summer hollered, her voice ricocheting off the lobby's stone walls as her hand flew to her nose to cover. "Where on earth is that God awful smell coming from? It reeks of... of..." She sniffed the air and gagged. "... pee! Did someone urinate on the floors?!"

"Yes." I pinched my nose closed. "Just hold your breath."

"Hold my breath?!" she questioned behind her hand. "Jayce, are you kidding me right now?! Why the hell—" Summer glanced around herself and in a lower voice added, "why would you bring me here?"

I pushed the call button for the elevator and the doors opened a second later, but even that was too long. Once the doors closed, the smell subsided and became less noticeable the further up the elevator car ascended. "I wish I could explain the situation downstairs but I can't. Just stick it out for a bit. I promise, you won't regret it."

She rolled her eyes away from mine, then pinched the innermost corners of her eyes. "God."

My sneakers squeaked against the floors and her heels clapped along the surface when we stepped out of the elevator and approached 8D.

"Well, at least the hallway up here is perfumed with food that smells good," she mumbled beside me. "It smells fantastic, actually."

I smirked to myself as we stopped in front of the rusted green metal door and I inserted my key in each lock. I knew if the setting turned her off, my mother's cooking would save the day.

The moment the door opened, savory home cooking greeted us and drew out a moan from Summer.

"Oh my God." She licked her lips. "That smells amazing!"

The evening news played on the TV screen as sounds of someone sliding pots back and forth over the stove's metal grates and meat being fried in cooking oil wafted from the kitchen.

"Take off your shoes," I told Summer. "My mother has a thing about us walking around here with our shoes on."

"Yes I do," my mother endorsed. She parted the faux crystal beads that hung over the kitchen entrance and stepped through them. "I don't like the street being dragged all up in here."

My mother's eyes locked on Summer, and a huge smile spread across her lips.

"Oh, wow!" my mother said with more breath than tone. "And who are you?"

Summer smiled. "Hi, I'm Summer McKoy." She held out her hand for my mother to take. "And you must be Jayce's mother, Mrs. Martin? I see the resemblance."

My mother had to drag her eyes off Summer to look up at me, her eyes never losing its wide form. "Jayce, she is just gorgeous. My God!"

"Hey," I said through my laugh. "You act like I'm some type of troll. Of course she's gorgeous. Have you seen me?"

Summer snickered next to me as my mother used her outstretched hand to pull Summer into a hug.

"Sweetheart, you can call me Mariah and please let that be the last time you ever try to get a handshake out of me!" She gently pulled Summer away from the hug to hold her at a distance by her shoulders. Her eyes moved all over Summer before she pulled Summer into another hug, this one tighter.

"Ma, come on." I groaned. "*This* is why I don't bring girls home."

"Shane, Shanae!" My mother hollered. "Y'all come out here and meet your brother's girlfriend."

"Oh..." Summer shook her head, tossing a glance my way. "I'm not—"

"His girlfriend?" my sister asked, exiting the bedroom quickly, tucking her phone into her back jean pocket. "You Boricua or something?"

"Bor-what?" Summer quizzed.

"She wants to know if you're Spanish," I clarified.

"Hispanic? Oh no, I'm black," Summer replied.

"You look mixed," my brother Shane said the moment he stepped out of the bedroom.

"You *are* very beige, baby," my mother said to Summer.

"Guys," I chimed in.

"Well my father *is* biracial and my mother's parents are both French Creole, but I assure you, I am very black. Promise." Summer held up her hand.

Shanae laughed. "Girl, you sure? 'Cause you don't sound black."

"Shanae," my mother scolded through her teeth. "Shut your mouth and right now. Summer, you hungry baby?"

Summer smiled while nodding her head. "I'm famished."

My mother grabbed Summer by the hand and led her into the kitchen. "The most high built your body perfect like a southern-born sister, so I know you like to eat. Come on."

I laughed to myself as I followed them into the kitchen.

It only took an hour for Summer to loosen up. My mother broke out a bottle of Alize that Summer was a little reluctant to try, but once my mother cracked the bottle open, Summer was gamed.

"So, y'all went to the same school together, graduated, and just started talking to each other?" Shanae asked.

"Summer told me she too good for me," I provoked, spooning rice and chicken into my mouth.

Summer's head twisted my way so fast I thought it would pop off.

"What?" I shrugged. "You did."

My brother, Shane, laughed. "Damn, you told him that, Summer? To his face?!"

Summer tucked her lips into her mouth, nodding.

"Oh, I like you," my mother and sister said at the same time before bursting into laughter.

"Y'all forever with the shits." I chuckled in response. "Whatever."

My mother, Shanae, Summer, and I retired to the living room once everyone finished eating. My brother, Shane, remained in the kitchen washing the dishes since it was his night to do them. Summer wiggled into a seat between my sister and I as my mother rummaged through one of our entertainment center's cabinets, searching for my high school yearbook, which she eventually found. Recent news about Pryce Williams possibly returning to New York to play for the *Bronx Ballers* came up in conversation over dinner. I told Summer I'd gotten his signature when he'd attended my high school graduation to give a commencement speech. I'd promised to show it to her. His celebrity hookups got the most attention, but he was a good guy that loved his hometown of Brooklyn and the school, Turner High, that gave him his start. I prayed the news was true, that he was returning to play for the *Ballers*.

While we lounged there, I watched Summer lean back in her seat for a better view of my sister's phone.

"Oh, no!" Summer told Shanae. "*Do not* reply to that."

Shanae's head twisted to her right to glare at Summer. "You're reading my messages?!"

I moved my lips to one side, nervous for where this would go. Shanae was very protective of her privacy, and understandably so. She was the only girl of my mother's children and she guarded her privacy like it was her baby, especially when it involved boys.

"My eyes fell on your screen and it's a good thing they did." Summer crossed her legs and positioned her body to face my sister. "Do not reply to him."

"If I don't, he'll just ask out Naila Lewis since she's been putting it out there that she's feeling him. He said so himself that he's thinking about—"

"*Ugh.*" Summer scoffed. "He would choose someone over your stunning self? Definitely don't respond to him then."

My sister fixed her lips to speak, but Summer jumped right in again.

"Never chase them, okay? Guys this young lose interest quickly, so why exert the energy that can be used on doing something more productive? Besides, chasing them is how your crown tilts, princess." She winked. "Do not respond to a message where the guy is telling you he's thinking about asking someone else out while he's showing interest in you. Let her have him if that's the case. But... here." Summer extended her hand for my sister's phone. "If you're *that* interested, I'll send him a message that will get him in line, promise."

Without hesitation, my sister placed her phone in Summer's palm.

I shot up from my recline in my seat with my jaw nearly down on the floor. "You won't even let me touch your phone to so much as check the time but you just put your phone in Summer's hand like that?"

"Summer sounds like she knows what she's talkin' 'bout. She's gonna hook me up," Shanae gushed. "Be more useful and maybe I'll give you my phone more often."

"Ain't that some—"

Shanae's phone chimed with a text, and what she read in the message made her hop up and out of her seat on the couch. "Oh my God, oh my God! You got him to ask me out?!"

Summer shrugged her shoulders. "I'm like the date whisperer."

Shanae giggled hysterically, grabbing Summer by the hand to pull her up and out of her seat. "You gotta come help me pick something out for the date. I like your style. Assist a sister!"

Summer turned to me. "Be back soon."

Just like that Summer fell into place, like a missing puzzle piece, and the shit was mind blowing.

"I like her Jay," my mother said, entering the living room from the kitchen and taking a seat where Summer first sat. "And she likes you too."

"Nah." I shook my head. "Summer's complicated. She ain't that easy to read."

"Baby, if there's one thing I know it's young women. I used to be one, you know."

I laughed.

"She likes you, *a lot*." She tapped my knee then added, "If she didn't she wouldn't have even gotten out of the car. I don't need for you to tell me that she's not from this side of Brooklyn."

A smile pulled at my lips. "She's not from Brooklyn at all. What gave that away?"

"She's got *Breakfast at Tiffany's* written all over her posture. The girl drinks with her pinky sticking up and she cleans the corners of her lips after every single bite of food."

A laugh bellowed from my mouth.

"She wears the same designer labels as the girls I saw you wasting your time with on *LU's* campus. But this one? Summer? She got class. The kind that's ingrained. Her speech is precise. She enunciates every letter in a word, and every single syllable. Little things like the way she eats has been well-curated. She's up there."

She nodded. "But despite y'all's differences, I can tell she likes you *a lot*. And I can tell you like her too... even more."

I leaned back in my seat and lolled my head over the neck of the couch.

"I'm in over my head with her," I confessed to the ceiling. "It's easy for me to pretend like I'm not when I'm around her, but it's true. I like that about her though, you know? Our opposites attracting. But I don't know. Every day my feelings for her keeps getting stronger, even when I force them not to."

"Tell her," my mother advised.

I sat up and turned to face her. "What?"

"Tell her that. Be honest with her, and maybe the next time you bring her here, your relationship won't be in so much of a gray area."

My mother leaned over and gave me a kiss on the cheek before standing up and returning to the kitchen to rejoin my brother in cleaning up.

"Aight," I said to myself. "I'll tell her tonight."

NINETEEN

SUMMER

Later that night, Jayce insisted that he walk me to my apartment's door. I wasn't expecting a trip to his old neighborhood, much less meeting his family. When he called me earlier in the evening asking if I wanted to go out and grab something to eat, I agreed because I'd been avoiding him since the previous Friday.

The conversation I had with my mother really screwed with my head. I needed to keep my distance from Jayce, so I only interacted with him at the office when necessary and sent his calls to voicemail when I was off the clock.

Tonight, though, I'd avoided him long enough and planned to tell him we couldn't see each other anymore. But the opposite was happening. After meeting his mother and twin siblings, Jayce had done something most men before him couldn't; get me to fall for him and fall hard.

"Thank you for walking me up," I told him once we reached the top of the stairs inside the brownstone.

He chuckled. "What's going on with you Summer?"

"I told you I was okay outside." I stopped at my door. "But you wanted to see me to my apartment door and you have."

Jayce licked his lips.

"You can go home. I'm safe now, see?"

He approached me slow and my breath caught in my chest.

"When have I ever just walked you to your door?" Jayce slipped my keys out of my hand and singled out the key for my top and bottom locks. "Plus, technically, you aren't quite inside yet."

He exhaled a shaky breath that brushed against the back of my neck.

Him this close as he leaned over me to insert my key in the door made me weak.

Finally unlocked, Jayce pushed the door open but didn't cross the threshold.

I stepped through, keeping my back to him. I stopped a few feet away from the door and inhaled two deep calming breaths. When I peeked at him over my shoulder, I saw Jayce leaning against the door's frame, his hands buried in his pockets, and him still not on the other side of my door yet.

I turned to face him, to find his eyes boring into me.

He arched a brow.

My mother's words poured into my conscience like coarse sand in an hourglass. Her forbidding me from seeing Jayce, wanting for me to have no involvement with him due to what her mind had created about his fictitious future.

My eyes feasted on him. He wore a simple jeans and tee with a *Yankee's* fitted cap turned to the back. His jeans laid slung at his waist. The tee he wore covered the waistband of the jeans, but I'm sure his boxers were peeking through. This was the Jayce I met in the halls outside my freshman orientation almost 5-years ago. The Jayce I'd fallen for at first sight. A truth I did my best to fight to appease to my mother. She'd invested so much in my future. Her advice had always been king. I'd be a fool to disobey her.

So, I'd end things between Jayce and me. I would have to...

... but not tonight.

I pulled at the hem of my white tank, slipped it over my head, and told him, "Come in."

With no hesitation, he stepped over the threshold, closed the door, and headed right for me. His arms circled my waist, which he used to bring me closer to him. The second his lips touched mine, I melted against him.

Jayce backed me against the nearest wall, the cold surface causing goosebumps to pepper my skin the moment my back kissed it.

"It's been an entire week since I've felt the warmth of Summer around me," he said against my lips. "What's up with that?"

"I wanted to talk tonight," I retorted.

"Oh, no worries." He smirked on my lips. "You're gonna talk all night into your pillow."

I lifted my chin and leaned my head against the wall behind me when his lips found their way to my neck. He licked and sucked gently, his hands caressing everywhere on me he could touch.

"What?" he whispered. "You don't miss me?"

"I do."

"You don't want me anymore?" He unbuckled the button on my jeans and slid his hand inside of them in search of my pussy. "She's wet for me, though. Just down here, drippin'. So I know you not wanting me can't be it either."

I gasped when Jayce inserted one finger, then another, his thumb getting in position to strum my clit too. My palms were flat against the wall when he glided his two fingers out only to reinsert them. He curved his index and middle fingers each time he slid them in, applying passive pressure to my G-spot as his thumb massages increased.

My moans traveled around us as Jayce pleased me with only his hands. In that moment I was his, and he was mine. Nothing else mattered, I wouldn't allow it. I needed this.

My lip was in the grip of my top and bottom teeth when he leaned into me to draw my earlobe into his mouth as he continued to stroke me with his fingers.

"I want all of you tonight," he whispered in my ear. "Mind, body, and soul. Can I have all that, baby?"

My head slid up and down as I nonverbally communicated my answer.

"Let me hear you tell me that, Summer."

"Yes," I whispered back, "You can have all of me."

On my bed, our clothes trailing from the front door to my Victorian bed, Jayce positioned himself between my legs and guided himself inside of me. He lowered onto his forearms so that our faces were only a few inches apart.

We kept our eyes on one another as he initiated his first thrust. He watched my reactions, studied my expressions, read me as my jaw hinged open and he moved even slower.

This was the slowest he'd ever sexed me. I experienced every inch of him that night. He stopped time with his patient strokes. At least it felt that way. Our breaths were both heavy, our bodies so hot and so close they could mend together.

"Wow," I exhaled, pushing the crown of my head into my pillow. "You feel epic... mmm."

"You feel even better." Jayce brought his lips to mine and kissed me. He rolled his tongue against mine while swiveling his hips slowly below the sheets. My walls pulsed twice around him and that made him go deeper.

Jayce gently broke our kiss and kissed me from my cheek to my ear. I lifted my hands at the same time I did my legs, placing each hand against his firm backside, his muscles contracting against my palm as he worked.

I pumped my waist to meet his dives, mindful not to wreck the flow. His pace never changed, but my body grew more and more sensitive beneath him. Soon, my breasts laid heavy on me, my body warm. That familiar pull from my pelvic floor, the one that always made me think I'd suck him into me, arrived and that pull was more potent. My eyes fluttered closed as I relinquished all control and just rocked beneath him, motionless. In these moments, I moved with him under his spell. Any and everything sounded right with us attached this way and with me spiraling toward a release.

"Promise me you won't give this to anybody else." He grunted each time he tapped my sweet spot.

I folded my lips in my mouth as I met my orgasm at its peak. I sunk my nails into his back to hold on. To continue to move with him so I'd crash like I usually did.

"I promise to give this only to you," he whispered. "Promise me the same, baby."

I shut my eyes tight when it hit and left me still. In my mind I repeated, *I promise. It's yours. Only yours.*

But those words took time to materialize. Instead, I clung to him and came below him. The climax light and fading soon after its arrival. He kept at it though, his pace quickening gradually until all that mattered to me was his dick sliding between my velvet walls. Those walls contracted again, this time faster, and soon my back bowed, and my body lit up with a need to come again.

"Oh, God, Jayce," I hollered.

"Promise me."

He slammed into me now. Jayce planted his hands flat on the bed, caging me in. He planked over me, working only his pelvis, the penetration so concise.

"I promise," I whimpered. "I swear."

Balanced on one arm, he lifted my leg with the other and fucked me until I yelled my release into my dark apartment, loving every second of being there with him in that moment, but also dreading tomorrow's sunrise because of what I had to do.

———

I came, but sleep never came that night. After another two rounds, Jayce and I fell out onto the sheets and he drifted off to sleep. I laid beside him, watching the sun come up, my mind racing with ways on how to break it to him... that we had to end whatever this was.

I was so deep in thought, I hadn't realized he'd woken up and had been staring at me.

"You didn't sleep," he stated below me.

I sat with my back to my headboard. When I lowered my gaze, I found him staring up at me from his reclined position.

"I got a lot on my mind."

His eyes searched my eyes for answers before I shut them in an effort to hide.

"Jayce, we can't see each other anymore," I forced out.

The bed moved a little as he slid closer to me, I kept my eyes closed because I just couldn't see his face in that moment. I'd rather go blind than to witness his reaction.

"Look at me," he demanded.

I slowly peeled my eyes open and focused on him.

He swallowed hard. "Is this about yesterday? Me bringing you to the projects? Because I brought you there to show you—"

"No!" I interjected, shaking my head. "Going there made doing this, this morning harder. Your family is the best, and so is your home. The visit was so amazing I forgot all about where we were. Besides the piss scented lobby, your old home was great. For the first time in a longtime, I enjoyed myself and I adore your family."

"Then what is it?" Jayce questioned. He brought his hands to my face and cradled my jaw in his hands. "Why are you telling me we can't see each other anymore?"

"My mother doesn't approve."

He recoiled immediately. "Are you kidding me, Summer?"

"She's made so many sacrifices. She has a vision for me and what my life should be."

Jayce was off the bed, snatching up his boxers and damn near diving into them.

"Everything she's done for me has been to set me up for the future she has had planned since I was in the womb," I added, moving to the foot of the bed to be closer to him. "

The least I can do is live up to her wildest dreams for me. She's my mother and all I have, Jayce. She just wants what's best."

"What about your fucking vision, Summer? Huh? What about what *you* believe is best for *you*?"

I gave no response. I had none.

He paused, getting dressed to place one hand at his waist and used his other hand to pinch the innermost corners of his eyes. "I'm curious; what doesn't she approve of?"

"Our differing backgrounds."

He shot me a disgusted glare. "Oh, but she's okay with fucking other people's husbands."

I jerked my head back and blinked repeatedly. "Excuse me?"

He shook his head and turned to walk toward my door where the rest of his clothes laid.

"No." I jumped off the bed, pulling the flat sheet with me, securing it around my body. "Explain what you meant by that."

"Summer, just forget it, aight." Jayce pulled on his shirt.

"No!" I turned him by his shoulders so he'd face me. "*What* do you mean?"

"So, you're gonna act like you didn't know your mother was your father's side chick?"

I grimaced, then scoffed a laugh. "That's absolutely ludicrous. My mother and father had a short romance, yes, but they were very much in love and he was *not at all* married."

"Yeah, okay." He snatched up his jeans. "You can save the fucking act now, Summer. Your father told me everything. About him fucking with your mother while he had a wife at home and your mother trapping him by getting pregnant with you."

I gasped.

His eyes were focused down on buttoning his jeans. "You know... the reason I brought you to my hood was to show you that regardless of where you come from, no matter how you came to be, you're here now. Your heart is your heart, and that determines how you move, not your background. But you can continue to play the perfect pretty princess role if you want to. Live your lie. Me though? I prefer living in my truth."

His words kept hitting me in the gut.

He had a wife at home...

I wanted to double over but was too shocked to even move.

Your mother trapped him getting pregnant with you...

"When did you talk to my father?" I asked, my voice quaking.

Jayce glared my way with narrowed eyes. He stared at me for a moment until the tension in his brows relaxed and his jaw dropped. Soon he lifted his hand to his mouth to cover.

"Oh, shit," he whispered in his hand, squeezing his lids shut. "You didn't know. That's why he told me not to—"

"When?" I asked again, trying my best to gather my breath so I wouldn't pass out. "When did you... when did you talk to my father?"

"Fuck." Jayce closed his eyes, then collapsed his head forward. "That following Monday after you two saw each other at *Sunny's Italiano*. You were so upset that night that I just... I don't know why I went to see him, but I did and he told me everything."

"You're lying," I whispered.

"Summer..."

"Tell me you're just upset and you're lying."

Jayce interlocked his fingers at the top of his head and looked away.

"Oh my God." My hand reached for the wall behind me to catch my fall. "I can't... I can't breathe."

I really couldn't.

The missing pieces to the puzzle began arranging themselves in my mental, drowning me in revelations. Everything that I thought was real wasn't. It all made sense in that moment. My father's absence, my mother insisting I do any and everything to make him proud, my sisters' disgust for me at the restaurant.

I was my father's love child.

"Oh my God! She lied to me. My mother lied to me."

"Summer, baby." Jayce crouched down in front of me. "Come here."

"No." I shook my head.

"I'm sorry," he tried, angling my head, so I'd meet my eyes with his.

I jerked my chin from his grip. Humiliation wouldn't let me look him in the eyes.

"Don't look at me," I whispered, covering my face. "Please don't look at me. Just, leave, Jayce."

My hands were up to my eyes when he tried to release them by gently pulling at my wrists.

"GET OUT!" I yelled this time, pushing him away. "Get the fuck out, right now."

"Summer—"

"I said to leave!" My lips trembled as the tears continued to fall and my eyes stayed fixed to my hardwood floors.

He pushed air out his mouth, then stood to his feet. Jayce crouched down for only a second more to place a kiss at the top of my head. "I'm sorry, Summer. I am so sorry."

That was the last thing he told me before he took giant steps out my apartment's door.

———

My fists pounded on the wooden French door of my mother's mansion no less than two hours later. It was still early, just after 11 a.m. when I arrived there. In a rare move, I'd driven home. I hadn't driven in a while, but there was no way I could wait for an *Uber* to bring me in my state. Doing over the speed limit, I barreled down the Long Island Expressway in a previously gassed up silver *Mercedes*, in route to her home to confront her.

"Mother!" I yelled. "Open the door."

I'd been calling her from the moment Jayce left my apartment, but she wasn't answering her phone.

"Summer?!" she shrilled on the other side of the back door. My mother pulled back the curtain on the door's window to peek out, then immediately unlocked the door and snatched it open. "What on earth are you doing here? And, lord, dressed like this? Your hair, my God, why is it so disheveled?"

"You lied to me," I spat. "You've been lying to me this whole time."

I pushed past her and stepped into the kitchen where she also kept the bar. It was before noon, but I needed something.

I slid glass bottles from left to right, hearing them clink together when she asked, "What in the world are you searching for, doll?"

"Alcohol," I cried. "Something extremely strong."

"Alcohol?!" She pointed over her shoulder. "You drove here. You can't drink and drive. Speaking of which, I told you to only drive if it's an emergency. An *Uber* is much more appropriate for visits here."

"This *is* an emergency, mother."

"Summer, what is going on?" Her eyes fell to my feet. "Are you wearing sneakers? Converses at that?"

I spun around to face her. "That has *always* been the one thing that mattered the most to you, huh? My appearance. How shallow. Like I'm really one of your porcelain dolls you keep on your shelves downstairs. I'm such an idiot for following behind you."

Her face tightened. "Summer, I will not tolerate your rudeness."

"Was my father married when you two conceived me?"

She gasped so hard her skin reddened instantly. "What did you just ask me?"

"Were you my father's mistress? Was I conceived while he and his wife were still married?"

My mother's hand searched for the back of a nearby chair. The moment she found it, she slid it out to plop into a seat.

"Because you told me that my father was single. That you two met at a party and fell in love at first sight. Conceived me three weeks after meeting but knew you were the one for each other until he left you for another woman and married her soon after instead of marrying you."

Her jaw hung open and her eyes moved erratically.

"It's all a lie isn't it?"

"Who told you that?"

"It would have to be," I continued, not answering her question. "That's the only reason he wasn't around often, that he never showed up for any of my events, most of my birthdays, why my sisters who I met for the first time last week would grill me like I was some terrorist."

"His daughters?!" she asked, her teeth bared. "When did you meet *them*? Why are you just telling me about this?"

"At a restaurant." My chest was moving up and down. "I was with Jayce. And thank God he was there because I would have been a fucking mess without him."

"Oh, please," she spat. "Jayce is just as much garbage as those two girls."

I scoffed.

"The only reason your father's wife had those girls was to spite me, to one me up. She refused to give that man children before I stepped into the picture because she was so obsessed with her medical career. He told me that you know."

"Mother," I breathed. "How could you do such a thing?"

"I would have given your father the world if he asked. All he wanted was a child. He complained to me about how selfish that woman was. How she refused to give him children because her focus was on progressing as a general surgeon. So I gave him one. He asked if I was on a contraceptive and I told him I was, even though I wasn't."

"Oh my God."

"I didn't *trap* him, I *blessed* him. And he worshipped you for the first year of your life. Your father purchased this house and was here practically every night to see you off to sleep until his wife couldn't take the thought of him finding joy outside of her home. That was her fault, not mine."

Tears streamed down my face. "I can't believe what I'm hearing."

"I wanted to shield you from this because you didn't need to know *this* Summer." She stood from her seat to approach me. "You got along fine enough without knowing. You've grown into a lovely, beautiful, highly driven and successful woman. Someone he is so proud of."

"Proud of? He didn't speak over five words when I approached him at the restaurant." I shook my head. "He was so horrified at the sight of me... because *you* got pregnant with me without his knowledge. Why *would* he embrace me?"

I ran my hands down my face and stepped back. "Everything I've ever done was because you promised he would be *so proud*. That was my motivation – this promise of finally earning his love, his approval, his presence - and it was all a lie. You've been *lying* to me this whole time. I don't even know what's real anymore. I'm not even sure who the hell I am after learning this."

"Summer." My mother took my hand. "I did it because I loved you and wanted to protect you. Look at you! You're about to get a job at one of the most prestigious law firms in the country—"

"I never wanted that!"

"You've *always* wanted to be a lawyer."

"Yes, a pro bono lawyer, or a lawyer for low-income individuals—"

"Oh, Summer, pro bono?! No way. And assisting people who can't afford a decent lawyer would pay pennies. Those options are simply out of the question."

"But I would be helping people who can't afford it, people who need it. People who deserve help just as much as those of us who can easily get help at the right price."

"I won't have it." My mother tilted her chin up and squared her shoulders. "No daughter of mine will ever know what it means to work for less than she's worth."

"You don't have a say in my life anymore, mother," I told her with tears in my eyes.

Her jaw dropped.

"That ends today." I wiped my eyes and stepped closer to her. "I love you, you're my mother and I only get one, I understand that. But mother, you no longer have agency of my life. It's mine, to live how *I* want. You have yours. Please leave mine alone."

She covered her lips with her hand. "Now, doll—"

"I was never happy living the life you planned for me. But now I see a way to live my joy."

"Summer McKoy—"

"Maybe now you can find love. Real love, and stop living in a made up fantasy of you and my father finally running away together and living happily ever after because that is never fucking happening mother, I'm sorry."

She exhaled loudly.

"You made me push away the one guy who showed me genuine affection, despite me being so ugly to him. A man who shows up for me consistently, and who I really love."

"Love?!" her voice quaked when she asked that. "Summer, no! Oh God, no!"

"He took me to meet his mother and siblings." I nodded. "They live in the projects."

"THE WHAT?!" she hollered.

"You would have thought it was awful." I laughed. "But it was endearing and beautiful because without that place, Jayce wouldn't be who he is today. Who he is to me."

"Christ," she whispered. "You've lost your goddamn mind."

I shrugged. "Maybe. But if I could lose it with him, I'd happily lose it every day for the rest of my life."

I turned on the rubber soles of my sneakers to head to the door.

"Summer, where are you going?"

"Away from you." I shook my head. "I'll call you when I'm ready to talk. Don't bother calling me though mother because I will not answer. I'm going to need some time to get to know me without you."

Her jaw remained slack as I opened and closed the door behind me.

TWENTY

The bottoms of my Italian leather loafers tapped against the polished floors of *Brown, Bloom & Associates* as I made my way closer to the conference room.

I hadn't called Summer ever since she kicked me out of her apartment that Friday morning. The sadness in her eyes broke my heart. I honestly thought she'd known this about her mother and was keeping the whole thing a secret because of her foolish pride. It tore me apart inside when I realized that wasn't the case.

When I slid opened the door of the conference room and walked in, my eyes landed on the empty seat at the opposite head of the table. Summer usually sat in that chair.

I took my seat beside Veronika, who had mastered the art of ignoring me. The only time she spoke to me was when we needed to work in teams, but other than that, she kept her distance.

"Okay, everyone's here," Jeff announced as he walked into the room.

My eyes focused on the empty chair again. I pointed and said, "Summer hasn't arrived yet."

"Oh, she won't be," Jeff stated. "Summer dropped out of the program earlier this morning."

A chorus of *whats* rang out around the room.

I stilled in my chair.

Veronika squealed. "There *is* a God!"

I turned my head to glare at her, and she shrugged her shoulders.

"So, now there were seven. There's always one that drops out before the 10-weeks are up." Jeff explained. "I'm stunned the dropout was her, but it was and now we must move on. Where are we with those revised cross-examination questions? I want to hear from each of you. Let's start with Jayce and Veronika."

I was so shocked by Summer abruptly quitting the program, it took longer than usual to register that Jeff had just called my name.

"Get up, Jayce," Veronika whispered to me before standing up and out of her seat.

The rest of the day dragged on. I tried reaching out to Summer first via text, then three phone calls, but she never answered or replied.

Suffice to say, two o'clock couldn't come fast enough.

When Jeff dismissed us for the day, I headed straight to the bank of elevators to exit the building.

"So, why'd your boo quit the program?" Veronika asked as she approached from behind. She stopped beside me and waited for the elevator car to arrive.

"I have no idea," I lied.

"Maybe now you can focus entirely on your role here even though I'm sure the job is mine."

I shook my head.

"Words can't describe how happy I am she's gone." She beamed. "It was a good day."

"You hate Summer that much, huh?"

"Yes, I hate her." She shrugged a shoulder. "There, I said it. It's not like she made hating her hard to do."

I leaned forward to stab at the elevator's call button. "My father once told me that having hate for someone is like you drinking poison and believing the other person will die."

Veronika blinked in response, but uttered nothing.

"If I were you, I would get my mind right and pour the rest of that poison out my cup because I doubt Summer is thinking about you as much as you're thinking about her right now. But that's just my opinion."

The elevator arrived, and I stepped in, pressing the button for the lobby and watching as the doors closed between Veronika and I.

Outside, I hopped in a yellow cab and took a ride to Summer's place, practically throwing my money at the driver when we arrived.

In front of the brownstone building's door, I rang her bell repeatedly and got no answer.

"Where are you, baby?" I asked myself.

She must have been so stressed because of me. I should have never told her what her father told me. Her saying we couldn't see each other set me off. Especially after I'd come to terms with my feelings for her being more than physical.

I ran my hands down my face then walked down a few steps lowering down into a seat. I bit at my lips in thought.

It was a sunny day, the sun rays dancing along my skin.

Dance...

"I used to practice ballet." I recalled her saying that morning before her mother showed up. *"I still practice it from time to time at Obsidian Sports Center in Brooklyn. My mother is friends with the owner's mother. They have a nice dance studio. I go there whenever I need to clear my head."*

I pulled out my phone and typed in the sports center's name in the search tab, then clicked out of the app and tapped into my *Uber* app to order a car to Brooklyn. It was worth a shot.

Twenty-One

Smooth R&B echoed off the walls as I twirled on the platform of my ballet pointe shoes. I swooned at the wind in my hair with eyes closed as I spun on one foot, lifting the other high enough to grab the vamp of my shoe over my shoulder.

I swayed with eyes closed, the vocal melodies and drums from Sade's, "Love Is Stronger Than Pride," shaping the surrounding vibe.

This was when I felt my most free, in a dance room, dressed in a pair of leotards, tights, and pointe shoes, being one with the music.

The gym's owners covered the room in mirrors and a long line of barres. I'd rented out the dance space at *Obsidian Sports Center* for the day. It cost me a few hundred bills, but I needed this. I hadn't visited the studio since graduating *LU*. So caught up with the internship... and Jayce.

The law internship at *BBA* was behind me now. It was a great opportunity that any law student would kill for, but I wouldn't have found happiness there. That was still me living for other people, and I'd decided to wash my hands of that completely.

I'd balanced myself on the platform of my shoes and twirled in a circle when my eyes opened and landed on Jayce, who stood at the doorway.

My jaw dropped as he stepped into the room, closing the door behind him.

"Jayce," I whispered. "What are you doing here?"

"That was beautiful," he praised a smile pulling at his lips. "You're really talented. I can't believe you quit this."

I smiled.

"Or Brown, Bloom & Associates."

"Yeah," I rolled my eyes away. "Neither can I."

He approached me slow, his hands hidden in his slacks pocket. "Imagine my surprise when I showed up there prepared to beg you for forgiveness only to discover you weren't ever coming back. That I would probably never see you again."

"And yet here you are." I licked my lips. "How'd you find me?"

"I remembered you saying this was a place you came to clear your mind."

"You remembered that?"

He walked up to me and pulled me close. "I remember everything you tell me."

I wrapped my arms around the back of his neck.

"Speaking of telling, I'm so sorry for telling you about—"

"Shh." I pressed my finger to his lips. "You will never understand how thankful I am you did that."

His brows wrinkled.

I inhaled a cleansing breath. "My mother did a great job of shielding me from a lot of stuff, a good deal of stuff. I needed to know the truth, and I'm grateful you told me. No matter how gut wrenching it was—"

"Summer—"

"Jayce." I smiled. "I *promise*, I'm okay."

"Oh, you keep your promises now?"

I laughed. "I keep *all* my promises."

We remained in that position, me with my arms wrapped around his neck and his forearms around my waist.

"I love you," I avowed to him. "I'm in love with you."

My eyes fluttered closed, and I dropped my head backwards. "I can't believe I just said that to you."

He chuckled and leveled my head with his hands, cradling my jaw. "I love you too. I'm in love with you too."

"I mean." I rolled my eyes. "Of course *you* are. Who wouldn't love me?"

"Oh, Ms. Summer McKoy." He licked his lips slow. "What am I going to do with you."

"I could think of a few things." I winked.

Jayce lowered his lips to mine and kissed me deep. Parted my lips with his and slid his tongue into my mouth, inviting my tongue to do its own little dance with his. He backed me against one mirror, his hand at my jaw.

I moaned on his lips, then broke our kiss gently. "You'll start something we can't finish here."

He glanced around himself and smirked. "Yeah, I guess you're right."

Jayce backed away, allowing me room to step around him. I tiptoed over to the chair nearby and took a seat to remove my pointe shoes.

He watched me attentively as I unlaced the silk ribbons from around my ankles. I blushed at the attention.

"So, what's next?" he asked. "Are you planning to do any other internships?"

"Yeah, definitely." I nodded. "There's this amazing non-for-profit organization, *Fair Law Society*. It was the place I wanted to intern my sophomore year, but my mother insisted I be patient and wait to intern at *BBA* after graduation instead. Now I'm going to do it. That's where my heart is pulling me."

"Good for you."

"I also would like to help a friend out who's been trying to buy a house for his family."

His eyes focused on mine.

"I have 8K, Jayce, sitting in my bank right now. I'd normally spend it on a ridiculous shopping spree but I know you could put it to better use."

"Nah, Summer." He shook his head. "I can't accept that from you."

"You're doing me a favor more than I'd be doing you one."

He stared at me.

"Your family is so amazing." I beamed. "Your mother is the best and so are your sister and brother. They deserve at least their own rooms. Your brother and sister should know what it feels like to have something of their own and a room, at least to me, is a decent start."

"Summer, I can't—"

"What? Are you now too *prideful* to take money from me?"

"Says the woman filled with the most pride I've ever seen in a person."

"I'm changing," I insisted, standing up from my seat. "Slowly, but changing nonetheless. Facilitate that change. Accept the money and put a down payment on the property. I personally think the job at *BBA* is yours, and so is the ten thousand dollar sign-on bonus, but why risk the wait? It's a wonder no one else has snatched up the property you're interested in yet. Wait any longer and they probably will."

He bit the side of his lip in thought. "Okay, I'll only accept it under one condition."

"Name it."

"Let me be your man."

My lips curved up and into a smile.

"Be with me. Help me put a name to what we got going on here because I've come to terms with it being more than just sex between us."

"That's it?" I quizzed as he wrapped his arms around my waist.

"That's it."

"You want to be with the uppity stuck-up bitch with daddy issues?"

He laughed. "Yeah, I want all that and more. It's like they say, the flaws are what makes the diamond sparkle."

"You're right." I balanced myself on the arches of my feet and lifted my lips to his. "And you're mine, and I'm yours."

My hands pressed against the back of his head as I invited him in for another kiss. This one dripped with passion, undeniable affection that made my stomach muscles quiver and my heart beat a tad faster. I'd contradicted myself by falling in love with a man I thought I could never be with. A man who went against all the attributes I swore I was searching for. He forced me to grow and to be me. And it felt so damn good knowing who I truly was, flaws and all, finally. Turns out it wasn't the acceptance of my father I was seeking, it was the acceptance of self I searched for. I may have lost what many would call a dream job, but I finally found self-acceptance and in the process found love and my dream guy too.

EPILOGUE

ONE YEAR LATER – AUGUST 28, 2020...

SUMMER

I stood over a simmering pot of marinara, stirring the sauce with a wooden spoon.

It was a Friday in August, my usual day off from the non-for-profit I worked at. The firm, *Fair Law Society*, assisted underprivileged civilians in need of law services without the means to afford it.

The job had become another source of happiness and meaningfulness for me. The first source, with that kind of power, was the man pushing his key into the door behind me.

I twisted my head to glance that way, and when I saw him I turned to face him.

"Hi, handsome," I said.

"Hey, beautiful."

Jayce had just walked into our condo we'd moved into just two months ago. Once our leases expired on our Manhattan apartments, we decided we'd move in together.

The prospect of Jayce and I living together thrilled my mother, if you can believe it. After our confrontation in the mansion's kitchen the year prior, despite my demand of not seeing or speaking to her, she was at my old apartment the day after apologizing with tears in her eyes. She agreed to brunch with Jayce to be cordial. Halfway through her mimosa and brioche French toast, she realized how great of a guy he truly was. Surprisingly, her approval didn't matter to me. I'd already decided he was the one.

Jayce and my place was a sizable condo in the upper west side. He would have settled for a spot in Harlem, but I insisted we get a place on this side of town. I begged him actually, and he compromised knowing that I'd made other sacrifices like willingly working a job that didn't really pay and that forced me to rely heavily on my trust fund my father established.

Our relationship, my father's and I, had improved. He called me directly every so often, and we'd go out for breakfast and lunch when time permitted. My sisters had yet to come around, one of them blocking me on social media the day I requested to follow. That was okay, I had my father's love, and that's all that mattered. Maybe one day my sisters would come around.

Steven McKoy was so proud of his eldest daughter though, he told me every chance he got. Ironically, knowing that meant very little to me, just like my mother's approval. These days, the validation I sought for many years finally came from within me.

"How was work?" I asked Jayce as I turned briefly to face the stove.

"Good," he replied, placing his briefcase down on the bar stool at the breakfast counter. He loosened his tie and continued to make his way to me. "I got my first solo project."

My brows wrinkled. "I didn't know *BBA* to assign solo projects this soon to second year law students."

With me out of the program, and secured in his heart, Jayce went full force competing for the only position available to the interns. Jayce's fresh ideas won over Jeff and the other partners, and they offered Jayce the job the day before his internship ended and promised to hand over that ten thousand dollar sign-on bonus 60-days after he officially joined the firm. He of course accepted both and had been flourishing at the firm ever since while maintaining an impressive 4.0 GPA in law school, like moi.

"There're whispers they're trying to prepare me to work alongside a partner. They liked my ideas for our case."

"Of course they did. Winning that Melissa Hatchett case with your bright ideas sure didn't hurt either." A smile tugged my lips up when his arms circled my waist. I leaned the back of my head against his chest. "Under this apron I'm wearing your birthday present to me, the one you bought me earlier this month."

———

JAYCE

I turned her by the waist and she laughed. I untied the red apron's string, and lifted it off her, revealing the white teddy I gifted her... well, that I gifted *myself* but *shh*.

Blood rushed to my dick, forming an erection in my slacks. I stepped back to check her out and blew air through my lips. "Oh, baby."

She giggled. "I figured we'd celebrate."

"And what are we celebrating?"

"Well," she started as she turned off the stove. "I got a chair at the office today."

My brows shot up. "A whole chair?!"

"A whole chair, baby!"

The non-for-profit that employed Summer was so small, funds would only allow for just a few desks and chairs. She'd been there since December of last year and spent more of her time out of the office attending court proceedings and hearings that a desk was never necessary. Plus, with law school studies and me taking up the other bulk of her time, Summer was barely in the office.

"And you know what that means." She winked. "I'm moving up."

"Yes, you are." I smiled. "I'm so proud of you, love."

"Thank you. I'm proud of me too." She reached for the cabinet doors to pull out bowls to plate the pasta. "Oh, and Ms. Mariah called. She wants for you to go shopping with her to help her pick out a good lawn mower. She wants to handle the landscaping of the house herself. Isn't that cool? I would have accompanied her today but I don't know a thing about lawn mowers or anything like it."

"It's cool," I replied behind her, burying my nose in her hair.

My mother and my twin siblings Shane and Shanae were finally settled in their new house out in Queens. A beautiful three bedroom property with a huge backyard with lots of grass. It was beautiful and perfect for my family.

"I'll call her in a few but I want to give you something first."

"Oh yeah?" Summer asked, her focus still ahead on the food. "And what's that?"

I'd been thinking of ways to do this, present my promise to her. Made reservations only to cancel them because I honestly didn't want to share this moment with strangers. I released her waist and lowered onto one knee, pulling the box out of my pocket and flipping it opened.

"This." I grabbed her by the hand and turned her to face me so she could see me down behind her.

Her jaw dropped.

In the grip of my hand, I held a blue ring box with a 1.4-carat round brilliant diamond ring set in platinum, sparkling beneath our kitchen's lights.

"Jayce!" she shrieked.

"I knew you were the one despite you telling me *nope* that day at your freshman orientation."

She laughed.

"But I was patient, and I waited for you to see in me what I've always seen in you but had no idea how to name it. I want forever with you and even more than that, and I'm ready to start here. You already have my heart, and I know I have yours too."

"You definitely do."

"And now I want you to have my name, so we can really seal this bond we have together. Will you marry me?"

Her bottom lip trembled over me, tears welling in her eyes. My heart grew full at her reaction.

She nodded repeatedly, then shouted, "Yes! I absolutely will!"

I folded my lip into my mouth as I slipped the ring down the length of her ring finger, and Summer couldn't help but to bounce up and down on the arches of her feet as I did it.

I laughed at her excitement.

"Oh, baby, come here, come here!" She grabbed my hand to help me stand to my feet. I bent my legs at the knees and circled my arms around her waist. I held her close as our lips came together like two magnets in a lip lock.

"I love you so much," she whispered on my lips.

"I love you too, baby," I told her, "so very much."

Summer lifted her hand with the ring high behind my ear and leveled it in her direct view. "Mother will faint when she sees this ring. Faint! It is so stunning, Jayce, wow."

"She's already seen it," I informed. "I asked her to go with me to pick it out."

"Aw, babe." She bit her lip. "That was so sweet of you to include her."

"Then she tried to plan how I would do it, and I had to leave her in the jewelry store."

We both laughed.

Priscilla and my relationship had ripened with time, especially after I landed that permanent position at *Brown, Bloom & Associates*. Her sudden approval of me didn't fool me one bit. Priscilla's views on me literally did a 180-degree shift when she found out through the grapevine that the partners selected me for the position at *BBA*. I didn't mind it as much. Priscilla wasn't half bad once you got past her shallow side... way, *way* past it.

"I'm glad you didn't listen to her," Summer whispered. "I wouldn't have changed anything about this moment. Not a single thing."

"I'm going to love spending the rest of my life with you, Ms. Summer McKoy soon to be Mrs. Summer Martin."

She smiled with her whole face. "Yes, baby, you are going to love it."

I laughed.

"And I'm going to love it too. That Martin surname is about to get a lot better with me wearing it, you know that right?"

I dropped my head back. "Oh, Summer."

She giggled. "Okay, let's eat."

"Oh no, no, no." I grabbed her by the waist, my hands sliding down over her derrière covered in lace. "I just proposed to the love of my life."

Summer blushed.

My eyes traveled down her frame and I moaned at the sight of her in that white lace teddy. "And with her wearing this, the last thing I'm thinking about doing is eating... food at least."

"Oh, really?" she asked with a sly grin.

"Really. Come on." I pulled her toward our bedroom. "Let me humble you more, show you what this married life will be all about."

She squealed when we crossed our bedroom's threshold. I picked her up by the waist and wrapped her legs around me.

"Tonight," I said, kicking our bedroom door closed behind us. "I'm gonna put it down in a way you ain't never seen your man put it down." I punctuated my promise with a peck on her lips. "Is that cool with you?"

"Yes, please. I insist." She smiled, eagerly sliding the straps of the teddy down her arms. Summer tossed her head back and whispered, "Humble me, baby."

THE END.

Author's Note

Dear Reader,

Thank you so much for reading the first book, *PRIDE*, from my *Love Is Cure, Vol. 1 – Vices & Virtues* series! This series was a long time coming and is my pride and joy, no pun intended... maybe just a little. When the idea to create a series that played on the concept of the seven deadly sins struck, I let it simmer for a bit. So many writers have tried their hands at the seven deadly sins and did excellent jobs with offering their takes. For this reason, I shied away from it because it's been done so many times. I got the idea 2-years ago, researched, outlined, threw away that outline and created a new one. Reworked it, still didn't like it, then put it to rest. But then I had a new idea to take the sin and find its cure. Hook the sin up with its opposite, create characters guilty of the sin and play matchmaker with characters who are divinely virtuous. And what came of it was what you'll read about in this series.

So, you met Summer and Jayce in book one – two characters from different backgrounds, but they found one thing in common, love. At the start of the story, Summer was too damn much, right? Stuck up, full of herself, and obsessed with the wrong things. She had her head in the game at an early age, I'll give her that. Motivated, focused, driven, and a go-getter... but for kind of the wrong reasons. Her mother tried to shape

Summer into one of the dolls she kept on her mantel. Is it a wonder why she gave Summer her nickname? Priscilla was obsessed with vanity, which is a byproduct of pride. Did you realize that Priscilla was fashioning Summer in a way to be appealing to Summer's father, Steven? Using Summer and Summer's successes as bait to get daddy to come home, which never worked? Yeah, that Priscilla needs an appointment with our resident doc Liz Peters because sis is so far gone. But Summer wasn't. I hinted at the good in Summer, the growth that was possible with a little redirection. It was necessary for Jayce to spill the tea and even more necessary for Summer to confront her mother. I'm so proud of Summer's evolution in this book because if she kept on the path she was on, she would have never found her true self or happiness.

Then there's Jayce – a breath of fresh air. Also motivated, focused, driven and a go-getter... but for all the right reasons. After the death of his father, Jayce took on the roll of being the man of the house while still maintaining a youthful spirit. All his choices were selfless, which is admirable. There's this theory that we all have multiple intelligences. I gave Jayce a good bulk of them and made him humble but aware of his worth. How did Veronika explain it? *"Smart but not obnoxious about it."* That describes Jayce to a T. What was there not to love about the man? Intelligent, expressive, family-oriented, and a bit of a hustler. He saw right through Summer's exterior and fell for her heart despite his initial intentions that weren't even aimed at doing so at the beginning. Jayce was practically the only person to penetrate the well constructed wall Summer, with the assistance of her mother, built. I think Jayce is one of my fave male characters. This is a man who is all heart, mind, and soul. This isn't the last you've heard of these two. You'll get an update at some point in the series, in someone else's story. All the stories in the *Love Is Cure series* are connected in some way, including the continued stories from my *Forbidden series*. I can't wait for you to see how!

Much like *PRIDE*, all the books in this series will be standalones and you can read them in whatever order you choose. If you're reading the books as I release them though, you'll read them in the preferred order.

I'm excited for you to meet the rest of the characters in this series. So excited, I included a bonus in this book... the first chapter of book two –

LUST. If you've read *Last Comes Love* and *Home For Christmas*, the name Pryce Williams will sound familiar. Well, this is his book. Enjoy!

But before I end this note, I want to thank you again for reading. If you're a new reader and you enjoyed what you've read, you're a Brookelynite now! If you've been reading with me from a book ago or many books ago, I thank you from my whole heart for your continued support. Please know I write for me and for your love of reading. See you at the end of the next book!

Love,

Brookelyn.

BONUS - Chapter One From LUST

LEELAH
Manhattan, July 5, 2019...

"So, Leelah, what's your sign?"

I rolled my eyes away from my glass and up at him to see an annoying grin stretching his lips. His name was Marshall, but in my mind I'd given him the name Martian because of his spaceships for eyes that he kept allowing to land in my cleavage.

It wasn't *him* that annoyed me, it was his type. White collar nerd. Very much not my type. Not that my preference was any better. If anything, I would consider this a step above the rest.

I sighed, wrapping my hand tight around the bowl of my wineglass.

"She's a cancer," my sister Gena said beside me.

She ran her fingers through her curls she cut into a cute asymmetrical style and that she dyed a honey brown. Gena was so nervous, and I couldn't understand why. Our dates were lames. What's to be nervous about?

This was her idea, this blind date. It was a double-blind date, actually. She met this guy on this dating app and he had a friend, Marshall, the white collar nerd. To make things less awkward between her and her dating app find, she invited me, her little sister to accompany her on this train wreck.

"And she loves moons," Gena added. "She's obsessed with them! She has a tattoo of the moon cycles that wraps around her ankles and stops at her foot."

I stared at her from the side of my eye and she tucked her lips in her mouth to keep from laughing.

"And she *loves* the stars." She grabbed my wrist and held up my hand. "See?" Gena gestured at the scatter of tiny black stars tatted along the webbing between my index and thumb fingers.

"Oh, that's cool," Marshall said. "Moons and stars are cool. Your hair is cool too Leelah."

I switched my eyes over to him.

"It's so bouncy, long, and curly. Just unapologetically wild! I love that. Reminds me of Chaka Khan's hair." He cheesed. "I like the color too. That brown and blonde suits you so well."

He tried so hard. Completely in his head and nervous. Sweat beads gathered at his temples and he wouldn't stop bouncing his leg under the table. If there was one thing I couldn't stand, it was an outwardly nervous man.

I wished he'd man the fuck up already.

"Thanks." I forced a smile.

"What about you Gena," her date, Fenton, queried. "What's your sign?"

"Oh my God," I mumbled to myself. "How much more of this must I endure?"

Fenton was less awkward. Handsome, if you liked the generic black ken doll type. You know the one, the kind of doll you find at the dollar store wrapped in wrinkled plastic.

"I'm a Libra," Gena answered.

"Oh, the lover of romance," Fenton replied. I'm sure his smile was visible from three city blocks away.

We all hung out at the Purple Cat, a bar so small, if you walked from one end of the room to the next, that would conclude your tour of the joint. It was dark in there, with violet lighting overhead. There were a few red, white and blue balloons and matching decorations still hanging around since the 4th of July was the day before. Our table was sticky and so were the patrons that came from all walks of life. From the 9-5ers to the habitual drunks. People crowded the place to capacity. All the makings of an establishment I wouldn't bother being in, but here I was, with my big sister playing wing-woman.

I leaned over in my seat and close to her ear. "Can you *please* go in the back and fuck Fenton so I can leave already?"

Gena snorted a laugh before bringing her glass to her lips.

"So... a psychotherapist," Marshall spoke again. I shut my eyes to keep from rolling them. "How's that job?"

I leaned back in my seat and tossed my hair over my shoulder while taking a deep breath.

"It's not a job, it's a career," I replied. "And it's rewarding."

Marshall nodded. "Oh. Right, of course."

My eyes moved around us, falling on the faces that made up my night. A couple in one corner had their lips busy in a lip lock, I couldn't help but to stare. It had been two years since I'd experienced even just that. I put myself on a dick diet a.k.a. celibacy on my 30th birthday once I realized using sex to supplement a broken heart was a juvenile idea, a detrimental one actually. Why is 30 the year we all want to get our shit together, anyway?

Now, though, I needed sex and bad...

"You've been nursing that glass for a while." Marshall pointed out across from me, pulling my attention back on him. "Did you want something else, perhaps?"

... just not sex with this guy.

I peeked down at my more than half-full glass and shrugged. "No. I'm not that much in a drinking mood tonight, Martian, I mean Marshall."

Gena choked back a laugh.

"We should order shots," Fenton suggested, his eyes on my sister.

"Oh that's unnecessary." Gena smiled. "I think we're good."

"Pryce Williams is making headlines tonight," the reporter's voice boomed from the overhead speakers, "and it's all centered on New York City and the *Bronx Ballers*."

The mere mention of his name stopped my heart. I snatched my eyes away from our table and focused them up at the flat screen mounted to the bar's wall, airing the ten o'clock news.

The reporter added, "Rumors are circulating in his camp that the *Oakland Flames'* center is considering playing for the *Bronx Ballers* in the upcoming basketball season."

"Oh, fuck yeah!" Gena exclaimed. "Yes, yes, yessss!"

I whipped my head in her direction and she immediately got rid of the smile.

"I mean... that *fucking* asshole," she said through her teeth. Gena tucked her lips into her mouth and held back a scream that still was audible to me.

My view returned to the screen.

"Pryce's two season contract with the *Flames* expired yesterday at midnight officially making the nine-time All-Star Defensive player an unrestricted free agent, free to sign with whatever team he wants. And according to insiders, he has his sights set on the *Bronx Ballers*."

"Is he crazy? Why the *hell* would he leave a franchise team for the likes of the *Bronx Ballers*?" Fenton asked across from us.

Yeah, why would he?

"Right?" Marshall chimed in. "They haven't won a ring since Lennox Walker played for them years ago. And before then it had been a decade since the *Ballers* made it to even the finals."

"Hey, be careful, now!" Gena warned, pointing at them. "Y'all better watch your mouths when you discuss my *Ballers* in front of me. I don't want to have to cut you for my favorite team in the league. Struggling or not."

Fenton threw his hands up in supplication while Marshall chuckled.

On impulse, I lifted my wine glass to my lips and chugged all the wine left in it.

Everyone at the table grew quiet instantly.

"La, take it easy," Gena whispered beside me, moving in closer. "Why does even the mention of Pryce's name do this to you every time?"

But I ignored her and her question. Didn't stop chugging until the glass was empty and I slammed the stem's bottom on the table below me.

"Uh, Fenton?" I called, out of breath and licking my lips of the wine that didn't make it into my mouth, "I'll take those shots now."

Book 2- LUST from the Love Is Cure, Vol. 1 - Vices & Virtues Series will be available Summer 2020!

About the Author

Brookelyn Mosley is a captivating voice in the world of black romance literature. With a gift for weaving heartfelt narratives and steamy encounters, she invites readers on journeys of love, passion, and self-discovery. Through her compelling storytelling, Brookelyn celebrates the beauty of black love and explores the complexities of relationships with authenticity and depth. With over 40+ titles, her stories resonate with true-blue readers, touching hearts and inspiring conversations about love, identity, and resilience.

Connect With Me Online!

Facebook: http://facebook.com/brookelynmosley
Facebook Reading Group: Brookelynites Book Lounge
Instagram: @Brookelynmosley
My Website: BrookelynMosley.com
My Readers Website: BKBookLounge.com
My Mailing List: BK Insiders